"Try not to worry about what happened tonight. I can't help but believe it was a random attack and had nothing to do with you personally."

"I desperately want that to be true."

She looked so small and so achingly vulnerable. Knowing he risked a major rebuff, he followed through on his desire and pulled her into his arms.

She sighed and then raised her face to look at him. Her lips parted slightly and he took advantage of the moment and covered them with his own.

So soft and so wonderfully warm... He touched the tip of her tongue with his and that was when she halted the kiss.

She reared back and he instantly withdrew his arms from around her. "That shouldn't have happened." She reached up and touched her lips, then dropped her hand to her side. "I shouldn't have allowed that to happen since we aren't even dating."

"Consider it a kiss from a friend," he replied, wanting nothing more than to repeat the kiss. "Can't we be friends, Miranda?"

* * *

**Be sure to check out the next books in this exciting miniseries:
Cowboys of Holiday Ranch—
Where sun, earth and hard work turn men into rugged cowboys...and irresistible heroes!**

* * *

**If you're on Twitter, tell us what you think of Harlequin Romantic Suspense!
#harlequinromsuspense**

Dear Readers,

Summer is winding down for me, but in Bitterroot, Oklahoma, summer has arrived, keeping the cowboys of Holiday Ranch occupied. However, cowboy Clay Madison isn't so busy with chores that he doesn't take the time to court Miranda Silver.

Miranda is a divorced mother of two children and the last thing she wants in her life is a playboy like Clay. But when somebody tries to kill her, it's Clay who runs to her rescue, determined to defend her against any danger.

The season is definitely heating up as passions flare and danger grows closer. I hope you all enjoy Clay and Miranda's story. It was a true pleasure to write. I just love the cowboys on this ranch.

Happy reading,

Carla Cassidy

COWBOY DEFENDER

Carla Cassidy

HARLEQUIN® ROMANTIC SUSPENSE

Recycling programs
for this product may
not exist in your area.

ISBN-13: 978-1-335-66190-6

Cowboy Defender

Copyright © 2019 by Carla Bracale

Printed in U.S.A.

Carla Cassidy is an award-winning, *New York Times* bestselling author who has written more than 120 novels for Harlequin. In 1995, she won Best Silhouette Romance from *RT Book Reviews* for *Anything for Danny*. In 1998, she won a Career Achievement Award for Best Innovative Series from *RT Book Reviews*. Carla believes the only thing better than curling up with a good book to read is sitting down at the computer with a good story to write.

Books by Carla Cassidy

Harlequin Romantic Suspense

Cowboys of Holiday Ranch

A Real Cowboy
Cowboy of Interest
Cowboy Under Fire
Cowboy at Arms
Operation Cowboy Daddy
Killer Cowboy
Sheltered by the Cowboy
Guardian Cowboy
Cowboy Defender

The Coltons of Red Ridge

The Colton Cowboy

The Coltons of Shadow Creek

Colton's Secret Son

Visit the Author Profile page at Harlequin.com for more titles.

Chapter 1

Miranda Silver was in a foul mood and desperately trying to hide it from her two children, who were running ahead of her on the sidewalk. Actually, she was exhausted and that always made her cranky.

Part of her exhaustion came from the fact that the high school students she taught English to had been particularly difficult and rowdy all day, as if in anticipation of the end of the school year that would occur in less than two weeks.

However, the real culprit behind her being beyond tired was her ex-husband, Hank. He had shown up at the house at one-thirty in the morning, drunk as a skunk and thinking that was the perfect time to fix the rickety front porch stairs of the house where he had once lived.

It was only when she had threatened to call Dillon Bowie, the Chief of Police of Bitterroot, Oklahoma, that Hank was finally convinced to go home. Thank goodness he hadn't awakened the children, otherwise Miranda would have really been angry.

"Slow down," she called to seven-year-old Jenny and eight-year-old Henry. Right now she wished she had half of their energy. She shifted her shopping bags from one hand to the other and tried not to worry about all the money she had just spent.

Last night she and the kids had gotten out all of their summer clothes and she'd been dismayed to discover nothing from the year before fit her kids now. So a shopping trip had been necessary and she'd spent way more than she intended. The price of new sneakers alone had nearly taken her breath away.

Of course, it would help if Hank would occasionally pay some child support, but at the moment he wasn't working and she couldn't depend on or expect any financial help from him. In truth, she'd never been able to depend on him for much of anything. He'd rarely kept a job during the last couple of years of their marriage and nothing had changed since their divorce a little over a year ago.

The two kids came to an abrupt halt at a storefront that sported frilly pink-and-white curtains at the window. "Mom, can we go in and get a treat?" Jenny asked, her big blue eyes sparkling with excitement.

Henry ran back, grabbed Miranda's hand and looked up at her with a sweet appeal. "Come on, Mom, we've been really good all week. We did our homework and made our beds and everything. Please? Please?"

Unfortunately The Cupcake Palace was a little pricey. "Yes, you both have been very good all week, but I just spent a lot of money on your new summer clothes." She hated to see the disappointed looks that settled on their little faces. Darn Hank anyway for never paying his child support.

"I'd love to treat a couple of cute kids and their mother to cupcakes and ice cream." The smooth, deep voice came from behind Miranda and instantly she stiffened.

"For real, Mr. Clay?" Henry asked. He dropped his mother's hand. "That would be totally awesome."

"Yeah, awesome," Jenny echoed.

Miranda turned to look at the cowboy who made almost all the female hearts in the small town beat faster.

Clay Madison was ridiculously handsome with his slightly shaggy blond hair and beautiful bright-blue eyes. His brown cowboy hat sat on his head at a cocky angle, and the smile that curved his lips not only showcased deep twin dimples but also seemed to light up the entire area around them.

"Evening, Miranda," he said with a gentlemanly dip of his cowboy hat.

"Clay," she replied with a curt nod of her head.

"Mommy, Mr. Clay said he'd treat us," Henry said. "Did you hear him say that? That's what he said." Once again excitement lit Henry's and Jenny's features.

"And how do you know Mr. Clay?" she asked her son. Bitterroot, Oklahoma was a small town but there was no reason her eight-year-old son would know Clay Madison, who was a cowboy on the Holiday Ranch on the outskirts of town.

"He came and talked to our class last week about being a cowboy," Henry replied. "I want to be a cowboy just like Mr. Clay when I grow up."

She was surprised Clay hadn't talked to the class about being a womanizer and a party boy. Rumor had it he did both things quite well.

"And I meant what I said. I'd love to treat you all." He gestured toward the shop door.

"Mom, please?" Jenny begged.

When Miranda hesitated Clay leaned toward her, his eyes sparkling merrily. "It's just a cupcake, Miranda," he said beneath his breath.

"All right," she capitulated, knowing to say no now would make her the meanest, most hateful mom in the entire world. Henry and Jenny jumped up and down in excitement. "Good manners," she murmured to them as Clay opened the door and ushered them inside.

Myriad scents greeted them, all of them good. The smell of chocolate competed with a sweet fruity mix. Cinnamon and sugar added to the mouth-watering combination.

Pink-and-white ice cream parlor tables and chairs beckoned people to sit and enjoy. Miranda stifled an inward moan as she saw the older couple who occupied one of the tall tables. Wally Stern worked at the post office and his wife worked at being the town's biggest gossip. Who knew what rumors would be whipping through the town about Clay and Miranda by morning?

Henry and Jenny danced up to the counter where cupcakes the size of small dinner plates were displayed. When you ordered one of the cupcakes you also got a healthy serving of ice cream on the side, making for a totally decadent dessert.

Mandy Booth greeted them with a big smile. The dark-haired woman was clad in jeans and a pink T-shirt advertising The Cupcake Palace.

"You don't have enough to do with the café?" Miranda asked Mandy. Mandy had bought the town's popular café several months ago and had opened The Cupcake Palace a month ago.

Mandy laughed. "The café is my bread and butter, but this place is my heart. I'd thought about opening some sort of fine dining place here in town, but Bitterroot isn't really a fine dining kind of place, and Tammy's Tea House already fills that need. Then I came up with this idea where I can bake to my heart's content."

"What does Brody think about you working all those hours?" Miranda asked. Mandy and Brody Booth had married two months before.

"Oh, trust me, I make plenty of time to keep my cowboy happy," she replied with her dark eyes twinkling merrily. "Now, what can I get for you all?"

Throughout the brief conversation Miranda had been acutely aware of Clay's presence. He stood so close to her that, despite the fragrance of the shop, she could smell sunshine and minty soap and a fresh-scented cologne that wafted from him.

"Hmm," Henry murmured as he and Jenny stared at all the choices, as if this was the single most important decision they would ever make in their entire lives.

"I'd like one of those blue cupcakes," Henry finally said. "Blue is my favorite color."

"Ah, an excellent choice," Mandy replied. "It's a cream cheese cupcake with blueberry frosting."

"And I'd like the pink one," Jenny said.

"And I'll bet pink is your favorite color," Mandy said.

"I love pink, but I also love purple," Jenny replied.

"Well, the pink is also an excellent choice. It's a rich chocolate with a raspberry frosting." Mandy began to plate the cupcakes. "And what about for you, Miranda?"

"Nothing for me," she replied. She wouldn't even be in here right now if Clay hadn't manipulated her into an awkward position in front of her kids. He could treat the kids, but she didn't need a treat from Clay Madison.

"Ah, come on, surely you want something," Clay protested.

"No, thanks, I'm good," she replied.

"Then why don't you and the kids go get us a table and I'll bring the goodies over when they're ready," he said.

"Okay," she replied and corralled the kids to one of the tables across the room from where Wally and his nosy wife Dinah sat.

She settled into a chair and watched Clay at the display counter. The blue shirt he wore was stretched taut across his back muscles and nobody wore jeans better than him. He said something and Mandy threw back her head and laughed. There was no question the man was a charmer…the town's Romeo. Well, Miranda wasn't interested in anything he was selling.

Clay Madison was the last man on earth she'd want to hook up with for anything. Hopefully the kids would eat their cupcakes fast and that would be the end of it.

She pulled her gaze away from Clay and, instead, glanced across the room to see Dinah staring at her and then leaning closer to her husband to talk. Of all the couples to be here at this precise moment, why did it have to be that particular couple?

"This is so cool," Henry said.

"We asked Daddy to bring us here last weekend but he said no. He always says no when we want to do stuff with him," Jenny replied. "He just mostly sleeps when we're at his house."

"And he snores really, really loud," Henry said with a giggle. "But Ms. Lori plays games with us and stuff. She's real nice."

Ms. Lori was Lori Stillwell, the attractive woman who lived with Hank in the small ranch house he rented. She worked from the house as a medical transcriber. She didn't seem to mind Hank's drinking or that she was assuredly paying all the bills. All Miranda cared about was that the woman was kind to her children when they were with Hank on the weekends.

Clay walked over with a tray that held the kids' treats and then returned to the counter and brought back two more. He slid a chocolate-covered creation in front of Miranda.

"I've never known any woman to turn up her nose at chocolate," he said.

"And you of all people should know about women," she replied stiffly.

"Ouch. I see my reputation has preceded me." The sparkle in his eyes appeared to dim a bit. "And you should know you can't believe everything you hear."

"What kind of a cupcake did you get, Mr. Clay?" Jenny asked him.

"This is a banana cupcake with rum-flavored frosting," he replied. "I love bananas."

There followed a conversation between him and the kids on what kinds of fruits they liked and what ones they thought were yucky.

Miranda listened to the conversation absently. She was just grateful that his beautiful eyes were no longer focused on her. Despite her intense wishes to the contrary, when he gazed at her she subtly warmed, as if he'd caressed her with his work-roughened hands.

She suspected that was his super power, that with just a look he could make a woman feel like she was the most important woman in the entire world.

She had no idea why he had decided to treat them all to cupcakes and ice cream, but if he had thought in his head to somehow seduce her then he had another thought coming.

She refused to be just another notch on Clay Madison's bedpost. There was no way she was going to play Juliet to his Romeo.

* * *

As far as Clay was concerned, Miranda Silver was not only one of the prettiest women in town but she was also a respected teacher and had the reputation of being a terrific mother.

He'd had his eye on her ever since she divorced Hank just over a year ago. For the past year Clay had been on a quest to find his forever gal.

He'd watched as his fellow cowboys at the Holiday Ranch had found happiness and begun to build futures with the women of their dreams, but so far Clay hadn't found the special woman he wanted to spend the rest of his life with. And he wanted that. He longed for that.

As much as he found Miranda extremely attractive, her ice-princess facade had always been offputting and had kept him from approaching her for a date. Buying cupcakes for them all was the perfect opportunity for him to break the ice and get to know her a little better. Hopefully, by the end of this time, he'd feel comfortable enough to ask her out on a real date.

"So, do you have big plans for your summer vacation?" he asked her.

She tucked a strand of her shiny blond hair behind one ear and picked up her fork. "The kids are involved in a lot of activities and that always keeps me busy, and I volunteer at the community center when I can." She met his gaze for just a moment and then looked down at the cupcake in front of her.

Being close to her was even better than he'd expected. She smelled like summer flowers and her skin looked so soft and touchable, but it was obvious she would rather be anywhere but here with him. At least she had begun eating the cupcake he'd bought for her.

"Is it good?" he asked.

"It's like a little taste of heaven," she said begrudgingly.

"Mine is delicious," Jenny said, her lower lip sporting a glob of pink frosting. Miranda gave her daughter a napkin.

"So is mine," Henry said. He wiped his mouth with the napkin Miranda also handed him.

"I know you work at the high school. Do you enjoy teaching?" Clay asked.

"I do." She stared down at her cupcake as if it was the most amazing object she'd ever seen in her life.

"You teach English, right?"

"Right."

Clay bit back a sigh of frustration. It was obvious she didn't intend to have much of any conversation with him. He didn't get it. He'd never done or said anything to make her any kind of angry with him. Was she this way with all men? He'd never heard of her dating anyone since her divorce.

"Mr. Clay?" Henry eyed Clay with speculation. "Do you know how to play baseball, Mr. Clay?"

"As a matter of fact, I do," Clay replied. For just a moment he remembered being young and on a ball field, the only place on earth where he managed to escape his father's wrath for just a little while.

The scent of fresh-cut green grass had replaced the sweet violet fragrance of his absent mother and a coach's pat on the back was the only nice touch he ever got from anyone.

"Mr. Clay?" Henry's voice pulled Clay from his thoughts. "Would you come over and teach me how to play ball better? I asked my dad to help me but he said he likes football and doesn't know anything about baseball."

"I'm sure Mr. Clay has far more important things to do with his time than teach you how to be a better baseball player," Miranda said quickly. She looked positively panicked at the very idea of Clay helping her son.

"Actually, I'd love to help you out," Clay said to Henry. "I could come over to your house a couple of days a week after school."

"That would be totally awesome," Henry replied.

"In fact, we could start tomorrow." Clay actually looked forward to helping the boy. Playing a little ball would bring back some good memories for him.

Henry's smile fell. "I can't tomorrow. We always go to our dad's on Saturdays and Sundays."

"Then Monday after school," Clay said. And maybe in helping Henry he'd have a chance to get to know Miranda better, and more importantly, she'd get to know him and not just his reputation.

He now smiled at her. Darn, but she was one fine-looking woman. The royal-blue blouse she wore enhanced the hue of her blue-gray eyes, and sitting this close to her he could see her long, beautiful dark eyelashes. Unfortunately, she didn't return his smile.

For the next few minutes he tried to make more small talk with her, but whatever he asked she answered with short, curt replies. All too quickly the kids were finished eating and they all got up to leave.

"This has been an unexpected pleasure," he said.

"It was definitely unexpected," Miranda replied. "Thank you, Clay."

"No problem." He looked at Henry. "And I'll see you on Monday afternoon."

"You promise?" Henry asked.

"I promise," Clay replied.

The kids ran ahead of them to exit the shop. "You don't really have to come over on Monday," she said softly so the kids wouldn't hear.

"I made a promise. You might not know this about me, but I never break my promises," he replied.

They stepped out into the warm evening air. "Thank you again," she said. "This was a nice thing to do for the kids."

"I like to do nice things. Good night, Miranda and I'll see you on Monday." He turned on his boot heel and headed in the opposite direction, toward where his truck was parked in front of the General Mercantile store.

He got inside his vehicle and headed for home with thoughts of Miranda Silver whirling around in his head. Being near her had excited him. There was something about her that drew him, but it was pretty obvious she didn't feel the same way about him.

He rolled down his window and allowed the late May evening breeze to fill the cab. The air smelled fresh and sweet with a hint of blooming flowers.

Clay loved spring, when the barren winter pastures turned a lush green and the trees once again sprouted leaves. It was usually the season of birth… cows calved and horses foaled and rabbits ran everywhere. All the cowboys had new purpose as they went about their chores after the winter's slower pace.

Fifteen minutes later he pulled through the entry to the Holiday Ranch. This had been his home since he'd been thirteen years old and had finally gotten up the courage to run away from his home in Fox Hill, a small town about thirty miles outside of Oklahoma City. He'd run to escape his father's physical and emotional abuse. He'd hitched a ride to Oklahoma City and had spent three brutal months living on the streets.

Luck had landed him here, along with eleven other lost boys, in the custody of Cass Holiday. Cass had passed away, but the ranch continued to thrive under the hand of Cass's niece, Cassie.

He drove past the big white two-story house where Cassie lived with her husband, Chief of Police Dillon Bowie. In the distance lights had begun to appear in the cowboy motel against dusk's deepening shadows.

The long building housed the cowboys in small individual rooms and in the back of the building was the dining/rec room. Clay parked his truck and headed around to the rec room, knowing that several of his fellow hands would probably be there chilling out after a day of work.

Sure enough, seated on the sofas and chairs were Jarod Steen, Flint McCay and Mac McBride. As usual Mac strummed his guitar, filling the large space with the sweet melody of a ballad. When he spied Clay, he stopped playing and put his guitar aside.

"Hey, man, what's happening?" Mac asked.

"Nothing much." Clay sank down on the sofa next to Jerod. "I just had cupcakes and ice cream with Miranda Silver and her two kids."

All three men stared at him as if he'd just announced he had decided to marry a cow and have the wedding on the planet Venus.

"You and Miranda Silver? No way," Flint said.

"Well, she is probably the last woman in the entire state Clay hasn't dated," Mac said dryly.

"Ha ha," Clay replied and then told them about the chance meeting with Miranda and her children. "I'll admit I've kind of had a thing for her for a while, so this evening was a great chance to get to talk to her. I'd really like to get to know her better." But there had been no way he felt that asking for a date would be a good thing when they were leaving the cupcake place.

"And does she have a thing for you?" Mac asked.

Clay thought about the awkward conversation and the subtle jabs she'd given him while they'd been together. "Definitely she has a thing for me. I'm pretty sure she hates me."

"Well, that's going to make having any kind of a relationship with her fairly difficult," Mac replied.

"The good news is Henry asked me to do some baseball training with him, so I'll be seeing her several times a week when I work with him," Clay replied.

"Too bad that kid's father is such a horse's ass," Jerrod said. A deep frown appeared between his dark brows. "Henry and his sister have participated in some of the activities at the community center. They are both great kids. They deserve better than Hank."

"Then all I have to do is convince Miranda I'm

not just another horse's ass," Clay replied. "I'll have to pull out all my famous charm."

"I know you're good with the ladies, Clay, but I have a feeling you can pull out all the charm you possess, but that's one lady you don't have a chance with," Mac said.

It wasn't until later when Clay was in his twin bed in his room that he replayed the conversation in his head. It was true that Clay had dated a lot of women, especially over the past year. But how did a man find the right woman if he didn't go actively looking for her?

All he could hope for was that Mac was wrong, because Clay really wanted Miranda to give him a chance.

Two hours ago Miranda had left The Cupcake Palace with Clay Madison. As usual, Miranda had looked perfectly put together in her black slacks and bright-blue blouse. Her shoulder-length blond hair had shone in the waning sunlight and she looked as pretty as she had in high school when she'd been the runner-up for homecoming queen.

She had to die, or at least be badly maimed.

She had to either leave this earth and be gone forever, or be crippled and ugly for the world to be right again. There was an enormous sense of satisfaction in finally deciding what had to be done.

Now it was just a matter of time and opportunity. The beautiful Miranda Silver didn't know it, but she now had an expiration date stamped on her forehead.

Chapter 2

Miranda woke up on Saturday morning feeling a little bit guilty about the way she had acted the night before. There was no question that she'd been rude to Clay and that wasn't really who she was.

However, there was something about Clay Madison that set her on edge. Maybe it was because she was far too aware of him whenever they were in the same space.

Okay, she could admit that she'd always been secretly physically attracted to him. But she also believed he was a fairly vacuous man, sliding through his life and women on his good looks and easy charm.

Besides, she wasn't interested in having a man in her life. Being married to Hank had soured her on the whole notion. She had given up her dignity and self-respect in staying with Hank as long as she had. Now she just wanted to be the best teacher she could be and raise her children to be happy, healthy and good people. She didn't need a man to accomplish those goals.

At ten o'clock the kids were in the living room with their overnight bags packed. "Do you both have your toothbrushes?" she asked.

They replied that they did. "And clean socks and underwear," Henry added and then giggled. "I knew that was going to be the next question 'cause you always ask the same thing before we leave on Saturday mornings."

"And then you tell us that you love us and we should be good for Dad and Ms. Lori," Jenny said.

"Great, then I don't have to say any of that same old stuff today," Miranda replied with a laugh.

A knock sounded at the door. Miranda answered to see her ex-husband, the boy she had fallen in love with when she'd been sixteen years old and had fallen out of love with after years of an unhappy marriage.

"Hey, Miranda," he said with the crooked smile that had once made her heart beat faster and now only made her sad. His eyes were bleary and red-rimmed, but at least there was no smell of alcohol on him.

"Good morning, Hank," she replied. She opened the screen door but didn't invite him inside. Beyond him she saw Lori in the driver's seat of Hank's king cab pickup and waved to her.

By that time the kids were at the door. A flurry of kisses were given and then Miranda watched as they all got into the truck and Lori pulled away.

Miranda closed the door and headed for the kitchen. On most Saturdays when the kids were with Hank and Lori, Miranda cleaned the house and then graded papers. Before she could get started on anything, the phone rang.

"Hi, Mom," she said when she answered.

"Hello, my lovely daughter," her mother replied.

Miranda smiled. She could imagine her mother sitting in her favorite blue-flowered chair, her silver hair perfectly coiffed and impeccable makeup highlighting her high cheekbones and bright blue eyes.

No one ever saw Katherine Albright when she wasn't completely pulled together. It had been that way when Miranda was growing up and even while her mother had been taking care of Miranda's father, who had been sick with prostate cancer for months. He had finally succumbed to the disease and was now buried in the Bitterroot Cemetery. As far as Miranda was concerned, her mother was the strongest women she'd ever known.

"I heard a little rumor this morning when I was getting my nails done," Katherine said.

Miranda groaned inwardly. "And what rumor is that?" she asked, even though she knew. God bless Bitterroot, Oklahoma, and its healthy gossip mill.

"I heard that you and the children had cupcakes and ice cream with that handsome cowboy Clay Madison."

"The rumor is true, but it was just a chance meeting. It didn't mean anything and it was certainly no big deal," Miranda replied.

"Well, that's too bad. You could do a lot worse than Clay. Not only is he easy on the eyes, but from what I hear he's a hard worker. Besides, he's just so darned nice whenever I run into him in town."

Good Lord, the man had apparently charmed her own mother as well as most of the other females in town. "Actually, Henry asked him to help him get better at baseball and Clay agreed to help out."

"If Hank were any kind of a father at all he'd be the one teaching that poor little boy how to play ball," Katherine replied and then went into a ten-minute diatribe against the man who had once been her son-in-law.

She harangued him for cheating on Miranda, for not being a good provider for his family and for not being a real and present father in his children's lives. She then went on to talk about Hank's drinking problem.

"Are you finished?" Miranda asked dryly when her mother finally stopped to take a breath.

"For now," Katherine said with a small laugh. "I just don't understand why a man with so much potential would waste his life."

"The good news is he isn't wasting any more of mine," Miranda replied.

"Thank goodness, and now to the real reason I called…are you planning on taking the children to the spring fling celebration this weekend?"

"I might take them for a little while on Friday evening." Miranda had put away a bit of fun money for the night where there would be people with booths and tents selling their wares, but more importantly for the kids, there would be carnival rides. "Why? Would you like to come with us? You know we'd love that."

"Actually, I'm going to help out at Halena and Mary's tent. You know they always get a lot of traffic, and Halena asked me to work with them and help them out."

"Are you sure you're up to it?" Miranda asked. Katherine suffered from rheumatoid arthritis that often flared up and severely limited her mobility. There were days she was in so much pain she was unable to get out of bed.

"You can't stop living because of a little pain," Katherine replied. "I'll be at their tent."

"Then we'll stop by to say hi to you," Miranda

replied. Halena Redwing and her granddaughter, Mary Nakni, always had beautiful paintings done by Mary as well as Choctaw-related items for sale. Halena was one of the town's more colorful characters and it was always fun to see what she was up to.

"You know I always love to show off my grandbabies," Katherine replied.

"And you know how much they love you," Miranda replied.

The two women visited for the next fifteen minutes or so and then hung up. Her mother always made light of the chronic pain that she suffered, but Miranda worried about her. Katherine had tried several medications to help her, but they had all made her violently ill, so the only thing she took now was an occasional pain pill to get her through the particularly bad days.

The rest of the day passed uneventfully. Miranda cleaned and worked on the pile of laundry that seemed never-ending with two active kids, and then all too quickly it was bedtime.

Sunday mornings she always went to church and hated the fact that her children weren't there with her. Lori had told her she was trying to get Hank to take them all to church on Sunday mornings, but so far it hadn't happened.

It was six o'clock that evening when Hank and the kids appeared back on her doorstep. As Henry and Jenny ran into the house, Miranda stepped out onto the porch with Hank.

"I hope they were good for you and Lori," she said.

"They're always good for us, but what's this I hear about Clay Madison coming over here to teach my boy baseball?"

"Henry asked him and he agreed. As I recall, Henry has asked you to help him several times and you always tell him you don't know anything about baseball."

Hank had the grace to look a bit sheepish. "Still, I'm not sure I want that particular cowboy hanging around here. You'd better watch out for him, Miranda. He's been known to turn a woman's head. From what I hear he's a love 'em and leave 'em kind of guy."

"Trust me, my head isn't in any danger of turning in any man's direction," she replied firmly. The last thing she wanted was to give her heart away to another man who might or might not take good care of it. She was just not willing to play the odds, especially with a man who had a reputation like Clay Madison's.

Hank pulled out his wallet and opened it. "The kids told me you bought them some new summer clothes." He handed her a twenty-dollar bill. "I know it isn't much, but this will help a little. You know as soon as I get some full-time work I'll make things easier on you."

"I know, Hank." If good intentions were cash, then Hank would be a wealthy man, but she'd stopped expecting much of anything from him. Still, the twenty dollars would help toward the carnival-ride expenses. "I'm planning on taking the kids to the carnival on Friday night."

"That's good. They'll have a great time," he replied. "They were both already talking about what rides they wanted to ride and all the carnival junk food they wanted to eat."

"They can ride whatever they want, but limits will be set on the junk food consumption," she replied with a laugh.

He smiled at her. "You're a good mother, Miranda. We might see you there on Friday night, but if I don't see you then, I'll see you next Saturday to pick up the kids."

"They'll be ready," she replied.

Goodbyes were said and Hank returned to the truck.

The rest of the evening passed quickly with baths and bedtime for the kids. It was only when she was in her own bed that she realized within the next four-teen or fifteen hours Clay Madison might or might not show up at her house. And she wasn't sure how she felt about it.

* * *

At three-thirty on Monday afternoon Clay showered and put on clean jeans and a long-sleeved navy polo shirt. A thrum of excitement rode with him as he got into his truck and headed toward Miranda's house.

On the passenger seat were two new ball gloves, a couple of baseballs and a good wooden bat he'd bought on Saturday. He didn't know if Henry owned a decent glove or not, but he would after today.

He was definitely looking forward to working with Henry. He'd forgotten how much he'd once loved baseball until he'd tried on a glove in the store.

Immediately he'd remembered the crack of a bat hitting the ball, the shouts and cheers from the parents who sat on bleachers and the joy of running full-tilt for a base.

There was no question he hoped there would be an audience of one for the practice today. He could imagine Miranda sitting on her front stoop while he and Henry played in the front yard.

They would be able to talk and maybe laugh together. He'd love to ask her out on a date, but he had a feeling if he did that right now she'd shoot him down quicker than a wild mustang could disappear in the pasture.

Still, the excitement ratcheted up a bit as he turned down the tree-lined street where Miranda lived. It was a perfect day to toss around a baseball.

The sky was a robin's-egg blue and the temperature had climbed to the mid-seventies.

He parked his truck at the curb in front of her place and got out. Her house was a two-story painted white with forest-green shutters. A nice wraparound porch sporting a couple of pots with colorful petunias added to the appeal.

From a distance it appeared to be attractive and in good condition, but as he walked toward the porch he noticed that the wobbly wooden steps definitely needed some work and the paint on the shutters was faded and peeling.

Before he could knock on the door, it opened and Henry bounded outside. Clad in a pair of shorts and a bright blue T-shirt, he looked ready to play.

"Hi, Mr. Clay. I'm so happy that you're here. I wasn't sure if you'd really come or not." He held in his hand a baseball glove that looked like it had been bought in a toy store.

"I promised I'd come and so I'm here. How about you trade that glove in for this one." Clay handed him the new ball glove.

"For real?" Henry's blue eyes widened.

"For real," Clay replied and looked just over the boy's shoulder to see if he might catch a glimpse of Miranda, but there was no sign of her.

"Like, it's mine forever?" Henry asked.

Clay laughed. "Yes, like, it's yours forever."

A lump of unexpected emotion leaped into Clay's

throat when the young boy threw his arms around Clay's waist and hugged him tight. "Thank you, Mr. Clay." He finally released Clay and stepped back. He put his old glove down on the porch and placed the new one on his hand.

"Does your mom know I'm here?" Clay asked.

"Yeah, I told her when you pulled up in front of the house."

"Okay, then let's get started." Clay couldn't help but be a little disappointed when he started playing catch with Henry and Miranda didn't make any kind of an appearance.

For the next hour the two of them threw the ball back and forth to each other. Clay showed the boy how to keep his shoulders positioned toward the thrower, how to stand on the balls of his feet and to keep his eye on the ball.

It was obvious to Clay that what Henry needed more than anything was practice and he hadn't even brought out the bat to see how well the boy could hit balls.

It was right before five when Miranda stepped out onto the front porch. She looked utterly feminine and yet professional clad in a pair of navy slacks that showcased her long, shapely legs and a white blouse that had a pretty ruffle down the front. Her blond hair sparkled in the sunshine overhead and once again he was struck by how pretty she was.

"Evening, Clay," she said.

"Hey, Miranda," he replied. He wanted to bound up to the front porch and sit in one of the wicker chairs there and talk to her, but there was no invitation for such a thing either in her greeting or in her stiff posture.

"Henry, it's time for you to come in now and wash up for dinner. And thank you, Clay, for helping him out." She turned and disappeared back into the house.

A wave of disappointment swept through Clay. "So, are you going to come over again?" Henry asked eagerly.

"Sure. How about tomorrow around the same time?"

"Awesome," Henry replied. "Mom is going to sign me up on a team soon and I want to be a really good player." He gave Clay a quick hug. "I'll see you tomorrow."

Clay watched as Henry ran up the rickety porch stairs and disappeared into the house.

The next day and Wednesday were the same thing. He and Henry worked in the front yard and Miranda didn't make an appearance except to call Henry in for dinner each evening.

Still, Clay was enjoying his time with Henry. He did seem like a good kid who was eager to please and showed a lot of gratitude to Clay. He also had a wonderful, carefree laugh that somehow touched Clay. Maybe it was because he'd been around Henry's age when his mother had left him and taken all the laughter with her.

Thursday when Clay arrived for more practice time, Jenny was seated on the porch with Henry. They both popped up and ran toward him as he got out of his truck.

"You said we were going to work on batting today," Henry said. "So Jenny is going to play outfield for us."

"I don't know what outfield means, but I'm going to chase the balls when Henry hits them," she said.

"Perfect," Clay replied with a laugh.

He didn't even bother to look for any glimpses of Miranda. Although he'd had ulterior motives when he'd first offered to help Henry, in the last couple of days it had become all about Henry and helping him to become the best little ballplayer he could be.

Clay was happily surprised to discover that Henry had a good eye when it came to batting. Jenny was kept busy running after the balls her brother connected with.

They'd been playing for about an hour when Miranda stepped out of the front door carrying a tray of colorful plastic glasses. Clay's heart lifted at the sight of her clad in a pair of jeans and a navy tank top. Her hair was pulled up in a messy ponytail and she actually offered Clay a small smile as she approached them.

"It's a little warm today so I thought you all could

use a nice cold drink." She picked up one of the glasses and handed it to Clay.

"Thanks." All of a sudden he felt tongue-tied in her presence. Jeez, he'd made small talk with plenty of women in the past. He'd been hoping to talk to Miranda all week, so why couldn't he think of anything to say to her now?

Thankfully she busied herself handing out the drinks to her children, who carried them to the porch and sat down, and then she gazed back at him. "A beautiful day, isn't it?"

"Warmer than usual," he replied as he caught a whiff of her sweet, evocative perfume riding on the air.

"It's really nice of you to be helping out Henry like you have been. He spends his entire evenings talking about you and baseball," she said.

"That must make you crazy," Clay replied wryly.

"It's not so bad. It's nice to see him so excited. You're helping him gain some self-confidence and I really appreciate that."

"He's a great kid and I've been enjoying working with him. He shows a lot of promise." Clay took a drink of the lemonade, pleased with the nice conversation they were sharing.

Henry set his drink glass down on the porch and ran over to where Clay and his mother stood. "Mr. Clay, we're going to the carnival tomorrow night. Why don't you come with us? That would be so much fun. Wouldn't it be fun if we could all go together, Mom?"

Clay wasn't sure who was more surprised, he or Miranda. However, he wasn't about to let this opportunity go by. "I'd love to join you all tomorrow night, but I think it's something your mother and I need to discuss in private."

"Oh, okay." Henry turned on his heel and ran back to the porch. "Now you can talk in private," he yelled back at them.

"I sure don't want to put you in an awkward position," Clay began.

"You mean like you did at The Cupcake Palace?" she interjected.

He grinned at her. "Without us eating cupcakes together, Henry wouldn't have a baseball coach."

"Touché," she replied, and to his pleasure her mouth moved to a half smile that appeared to hold a touch of warmth.

"Miranda, I would love to take you all to the carnival tomorrow night," he continued. "It's never much fun to go to those kinds of things alone."

The warmth he'd thought he saw in her eyes seemed to frost just a bit. "I'm sure if you really wanted to, you could find somebody to go with you."

"That may be true, but there's nothing better than enjoying a carnival with a couple of kids," he replied. He glanced over to where Jenny and Henry sat on the porch and then looked back at her. "Please allow me the pleasure of taking you and the kids to-morrow night."

Although he hadn't thought much about the big festivities starting the next night until Henry mentioned it, more than anything at this moment he wanted Miranda to say they would all go together. He held his breath as he waited for her to reply.

She looked toward the kids and then gazed back at him. "It wouldn't be a date," she finally said.

"Of course not," he replied hurriedly.

"Because I don't date."

"Okay, then it would just be an evening of us all hanging out together," he assured her. "Besides, I promise to ride all the scary rides with Henry."

"Ha, you would be riding those rides with Jenny. She's my little daredevil." She stared at him for a long moment and then slowly nodded her head. "Okay, we'll go with you as long as you understand it's all about the kids and this has nothing to do with you and me having any kind of a relationship."

"I completely understand." Clay tamped down his elation. "What time should I be here to pick you all up?"

"Why don't we make it around six? And we'll want to stay until after dark. The kids always like seeing all the carnival lights."

"That's part of the fun. Then six it is." He looked over to Henry and Jenny who were still seated on the porch. "We're all going to the carnival together tomorrow night."

"Awesome," Henry yelled as he jumped off the porch and raced toward them.

Jenny was right behind him, her pretty little features lit with happiness. "Do you like scary rides, Mr. Clay?" she asked.

"I do," he replied. "Scary rides are some of my favorites."

"Oh, good, because Mommy and Henry don't like them. They're just two old fraidy-cats."

"Then I'll be your scary ride buddy." Clay laughed as the little girl clapped her hands together and her blond ponytail danced up and down.

"And do you like funnel cake?" Henry asked.

Clay laughed again. "I love funnel cake."

"Only after you eat something better for dinner," Miranda said. "We'll get hot dogs or something for dinner before any funnel cake is allowed."

"Speaking of dinner... I'd better get back to the ranch before Cookie puts everything away," he said. Cord Cully, aka Cookie, was the cantankerous old man who provided the meals to all the cowboys at the Holiday Ranch. "I'll see you all tomorrow at six."

Minutes later, as Clay headed for home, more than a bit of excitement danced through his veins. No matter what Miranda called it, tomorrow night he was going to have his first date with her.

Chapter 3

Okay, she'd had a weak moment. That was the only way to explain Miranda's agreement to go with Clay to the carnival. When he'd told her he'd like to take them all and that there was nothing better than enjoying a carnival with kids, she'd thought she saw a whisper of loneliness in his eyes. And that, coupled with all his work with Henry, had made for a weak moment.

Throughout the day on Friday she fought the impulse to pick up the phone and call or text him and cancel the evening plans. It would certainly be the smart thing to do, but ultimately she hadn't made the call.

It didn't help that Henry and Jenny were so excited about sharing the evening with him. They'd not only talked about it all yesterday evening but now at five-thirty they had already parked themselves at the front window to wait for his arrival. If she'd canceled the plans with Clay they would have been bitterly disappointed.

There would be a lot of speculation when people saw them all together. People were definitely going to talk, but she was used to that. She had often been the topic of town gossip when she'd been married to Hank.

She now focused her attention on the bathroom mirror. It was supposed to be a little cool this evening so she'd opted to wear jeans, a light blue short-sleeved blouse and a white cardigan sweater.

She didn't know if she was dreading or looking forward to the night. Certainly she was looking forward to seeing Henry and Jenny having fun. And it wasn't as if she was really dreading spending time with Clay. She was just cautious…very, very cautious.

Every afternoon when he had arrived to work with Henry, she'd spent a long time hiding behind the curtains in the living room and watching out the window as Clay interacted with her son.

The first thing she'd noticed was how Clay's shirt stretched across his muscled back and broad shoulders, and how his jeans clung to his butt and long legs. Yes, the man was definitely hot.

What was even hotter was how often he had praised Henry and how patient he was with the little boy. There was also a lot of laughter between the two during the practices. It was hard to dislike a man with those kinds of attributes.

For Henry and Jenny's sake, she'd put up with Clay's presence with them tonight, but there would be no more social activities between them in the future. The last thing she wanted in her life again was a party boy who loved the women. Been there… done that…and she never, ever wanted to do it again.

She left her bedroom and went into the living room to wait for Clay's arrival. As they waited, the conversation revolved around cotton candy and funnel cake and fun rides. It had been a long time since she'd seen her children so excited about a night out and at least part of that excitement came from Clay's going with them.

"There's going to be a big crowd at the carnival, so it's really important that we all stay together," Miranda said. "That means no running off for anything. Do you both understand?"

The two of them nodded. She wanted to make sure they knew this rule before they got to the festivities. Jenny was especially guilty of often wandering off or running ahead.

At exactly six o'clock Miranda couldn't help

the unexpected butterflies that took wing in the pit of her stomach when Clay's bright blue king-cab pickup pulled up in the driveway. She grabbed her purse and corralled the kids outside before he could even step out of his vehicle.

"Hey." He greeted them with that smile that flashed his dimples and seemed to brighten the air around him. "Are you all ready for some fun?"

"Definitely," she said, but her voice was drowned out by Henry and Jenny shouting with their excitement.

It took only minutes to get the kids settled in the back and her in the passenger seat. She was definitely ready for some fun. It had been a long week with her students stressed over finals and acting out in ridiculous ways.

"You look mighty pretty," he said as he started the truck.

"Thank you." He looked mighty fine himself, clad in jeans and a black long-sleeved polo shirt that clung to his muscles and enhanced his blond hair. He smelled good, too. The fragrance of minty soap and a clean, fresh cologne wafted from him and filled the interior of the truck.

"I hope you don't mind, but when we first get there I'd like to find Halena and Mary's booth," she said. "My mother is helping them out tonight and wanted us all to stop by."

"That's not a problem. I always enjoy visiting

with your mom, and Halena is usually a real hoot," he replied.

As they traveled to the old rodeo grounds just on the outskirts of town, the conversation remained light. Miranda felt herself beginning to relax, although the butterflies continued to swirl in the pit of her stomach each time she glanced at him.

Of all the men in Bitterroot, why did Clay Madison have to be the one to give her butterflies? He was the antithesis of what she wanted in a man... if she'd been in the market for a man...which she wasn't.

She was grateful when they reached the fairgrounds where the musical sound of the carousal battled with the barkers who urged people to throw a ball or flip a ring or toss a dart for a big prize.

The scents of cotton candy, sizzling hot dogs and freshly popped popcorn rode the evening air. The sounds and the smells made any deep thoughts impossible.

"Will you ride the carousal with me, Mr. Clay?" Henry asked as they walked toward the festivities. "I want to ride it and pretend I'm a cowboy riding the range."

Clay laughed and threw his arm around Henry's shoulders. "I'd be honored to ride with you, partner."

It should be Hank throwing his arm around his son, Miranda thought, but Hank would rather wrap his arms around a bottle of gin. However, Miranda had long ago become resigned to Hank's shortcomings and she tried to be both mother and father to her kids.

Still, she didn't want her son to get too close to Clay. She didn't want Henry to get hurt by any man. It was bad enough that Hank continued to disappoint his son on a regular basis.

Although she would love for Henry to have a good, strong male role model in his life, there was no way that man would be Romeo Clay Madison.

As they joined the throngs of people, she couldn't help but remember all the reasons she was wary of Clay and his reputation.

"Evening, Clay," Bonnie Abrahams said from their left as they walked toward Mary and Halena's booth. Bonnie toyed with a strand of her long, bleached hair and batted her false eyelashes. "Miranda," she added with another flip of her hair.

"Hi, Bonnie," Clay replied with his easy smile. "Did you ever get that old car up and running?"

"Larry down at the garage fixed me up and it's now purring like a kitten," Bonnie said.

Clay turned to Miranda. "Bonnie has a sweet 1969 Mustang convertible. I tried to help get it running for her." He grinned ruefully. "I can easily rope a cow, but I'm sure no mechanic."

"Still, you know I really appreciated you trying to help me out," Bonnie replied.

As they continued on their way to Mary and

Halena's booth, Clay was greeted by more women. "Is there any female in this town you don't know?" Miranda finally asked.

Clay laughed. "I'm sure there are a few. What can I say? I spend a lot of time in town when I'm not working on the ranch. I hang out at the café or at the Watering Hole and so I meet a lot of people. And I'm sure I know as many men as I do women." He flashed his charming smile. "I'm a friendly kind of guy."

Thankfully, by that time they had reached Mary and Halena's booth. The kids ran toward Miranda's mother, who embraced them both in a group hug.

Mary looked first at Miranda and then at Clay, her beautiful features radiating more than a touch of surprise. Clay greeted her with a hug and then approached Halena and hugged her, as well.

"And aren't you two a surprise," Halena said. "Clay, you'd better treat her right. She's a good woman." Halena reached up and straightened her hat, a creation of pink and red silk flowers with a miniature Ferris wheel among the blooms. The Choctaw woman was known for her outlandish hats, among other things.

"Oh, it isn't like that," Miranda said hurriedly. "Clay has been helping Henry with baseball and he really wanted Clay to come with us tonight, but Clay and I…we aren't together. It's nothing like that."

"Hmm, too bad. You make a good-looking couple," Halena replied. "I'm still waiting for the man who will make me part of a good-looking couple. But you two really should be a couple." She turned on her moccasins and began to straighten a rack full of colorful clothing.

"How's business?" Miranda asked Mary, eager for a change of topic.

"As you can see, it's a little slow right now, but tomorrow will be our big day," she replied. "Still, it should pick up some in the next couple of hours or so."

"We'd better sell a lot because I need some new hats," Halena said.

Mary rolled her eyes. "My grandmother needs a new hat like I need a pet pig."

"Can we get a pet pig, Mom?" Henry asked.

"Absolutely not," Miranda replied.

"Can we get a dog?" he asked.

Miranda shook her head. "Not right now."

"Then can we go get some hot dogs? I'm starving."

She laughed. "That we can do."

They said their goodbyes to Mary, Halena and Miranda's mother, and then they headed for the closest place to get something to eat.

The crowd had grown while they'd been visiting. They were almost to the hot dog booth when they ran into Hank and Lori. "Daddy!" The kids greeted him by running to him and hugging him.

"What have we here?" Hank asked as his gaze shot from Miranda to Clay. Miranda could tell he'd been drinking, not only by the bleary look in his eyes but also by the gruff belligerence in his voice. "I warned you about this cowboy, Miranda. What in the hell are you doing here with him?"

"Hank, whatever issues you have with me...now is not the time," Clay replied calmly. He looked pointedly at the two kids, who had crept closer to Miranda's side.

Lori grabbed Hank's arm. "Come on, Hank. You promised me a ride on the Ferris wheel. Let's go take that ride."

Hank grumbled beneath his breath and glared at them one more time, and then thankfully Lori managed to pull him away.

"Come on, kids. Let's go get some hot dogs," Clay said, breaking the tension with his easy grin.

Miranda smiled at him, grateful that he hadn't gone all macho and added to what could have been a difficult situation with Hank. Within minutes Hank was forgotten as they all sat at a picnic table with juicy hot dogs and crispy french fries before them.

"So, what are we going to ride first?" Clay asked as they were finishing up the meal.

"The octopus," Jenny said.

"The carousel," Henry replied.

"And what would you like to ride?" Clay asked Miranda.

"I'm kind of like my son…nothing too fast or too scary. I think it would be fun for all of us to ride the bumper cars," she replied.

His eyes lit up. "What do you say, kids? How about we all bump your mother?"

"Yes," Henry replied and fist-pumped in the air.

"Don't worry, Mommy. I'm on your side and I'm going to bump Mr. Clay really hard," Jenny said.

Challenges were thrown down amid laughter and that seemed to set the mood for fun. For the next hour they enjoyed a variety of rides and then took a break for funnel cake.

"I love funnel cake," Henry said with the lower half of his face covered in powdered sugar. "I think it's my favorite dessert in the whole world. What's your favorite dessert, Mr. Clay?"

"I like mud pies," he replied, making them all laugh.

"I like to make mud pies," Jenny said, and then giggled. "But I don't ever eat them."

"Thank goodness," Miranda said with a laugh.

After the sweet treat it was time for them to ride the carousel. Henry chose a white horse with a lei of blue flowers around its neck and Clay climbed on the brown one next to him. Miranda and Jenny took the horses right behind them.

As the music began and the carousel started to move, Miranda was surprised to realize she was having fun…she was having lots of fun with Clay.

He was a charming tease and made her and the kids laugh. Although any real conversation was tough with the music and the noise of the crowd, what they had shared had been so natural and easy.

It was strange; she didn't believe he was consciously seducing her and yet she somehow felt seduced. She watched now as he leaned over his horse, as if pretending to spur it to run faster. Henry laughed in delight and also leaned over his horse.

That was part of his seduction, that he was so good with the kids. His enjoyment of them appeared to be one hundred percent genuine and it was obvious they adored him.

His beautiful eyes often lit with laughter and he had one of those smiles that made it almost impossible not to smile back.

She was appalled to recognize that she was even more sexually attracted to him than she had been. Of course, it had been almost two years since she'd been with a man. She'd stopped having sex with Hank almost a year before they had divorced.

Clay was a very sexy, handsome cowboy. Why wouldn't she be sexually attracted to him? That certainly didn't mean she was going to act on that attraction.

"How about we go see if Henry and I can win a couple of stuffed animals for the ladies?" Clay asked as they got off the carousel.

"That sounds like fun!" Henry replied. "Can we, Mom?"

Her intention had been to skip the games of chance, but she wound up capitulating to the majority. They had just about made it to those particular booths when three familiar teenagers bumped into them.

Jason Rogers, Robby Davies, and Glen Thompson were all seniors. They were big guys with a penchant for bullying younger and smaller kids at the school.

"Hey, chill out," Clay said as they all shoulder-bumped, jostling Jason into Henry.

"Well, if it isn't strait-laced Silver," Robby said. His friends laughed as if he'd said something amazingly funny.

Miranda's cheeks burned with a touch of embarrassment. She'd known that some of the boys at school called her that behind her back, but this was the first time it had been said to her face.

"Wise guy, it might not be so smart to bad-talk a teacher during finals," Clay said.

"Ha, the joke is on you, you dumb cowboy. I'm not in any of her classes," Robby replied, his tone filled with an utter disrespect that surprised her.

"Come on, Robby," Jason said, as if sensing the tension that was suddenly in the air and wafting off Clay.

"Yeah, man, let's go. I'm starving," Glen added.

"Do I smell beer on your breaths?" Miranda asked. She was sure she smelled booze.

"Underage drinking is a serious offense," Clay added. "Maybe we all need to go find Chief Bowie."

"Let's go," Glen said. "I don't want to get in any trouble. My dad would kill me."

"I suggest you all move on," Clay replied. His voice held a hard edge. "But before you go, I believe you owe Ms. Silver an apology."

Robby's eyes held a hint of anger. He opened his mouth and then snapped it shut. He shoved his hands in his pockets and looked down at his feet. "Sorry," he said, his voice a surly snarl.

"And Robby, a word of advice…be careful who you call a dumb cowboy in this town. One of those dumb cowboys just might wind up giving you a butt-whipping you'll never forget."

Clay held Robby's gaze until finally Robby looked away. "Come on, guys. We've got more important things to do than waste our time here," he said.

"What a piece of work," Clay said as the three disappeared into the crowd.

"I think they all were booze-brave. I've never seen Robby be so disrespectful."

"Let's just forget about them." Clay threw his arm around her shoulders and looked at the kids. "Come on, let's go win some stuffed animals."

She told herself she should step away from him

and dislodge his arm from around her. But the night was cool and his arm was so very warm—and there was nothing even vaguely sexual about it.

In any case, he was the one who withdrew his arm when they reached the first booth. You had to shoot water into a target to fill a balloon, and he insisted they all play.

Their competitive sides were definitely on display as they hooted and hollered in an effort to distract each other. In the end Clay won and his prize was a flashy plastic bracelet that he gave to Jenny.

"That was just for a warm-up," he said and gestured toward the next booth where stuffed animals hung from hooks overhead. Poodles and tigers, baby elephants and bears all challenged them to take one home.

By the time the night was over, both Jenny and Henry held stuffed bears in their arms. Miranda's stomach hurt from laughing so much. Her belly was full of carnival food and even though she didn't really know Clay any better than she had before, she felt a strange kind of closeness to him...a connection forged in laughter and fun.

And they'd had fun. She'd enjoyed his company and that was why she didn't want to put herself in this kind of position again with him. He could finish up helping Henry with baseball, but that was it.

Once again, as they headed down the midway in the direction of the parking area in the distance, they were elbowed and bumped by the crowd. The carnival's illumination made everything a beautiful color against the darkness of the night.

They paused to turn back and admire the many colored lights that outlined the Ferris wheel rising up in the dark sky and every other ride along the midway. The kids oohed and aahed over the lights, but she could tell both of them were getting tired. It had been a long evening for them.

They turned back to continue their trek to the car. A hard push moved Miranda sideways and at the same time something splashed all over the front of her sweater. Darn, somebody had spilled a drink on her. She stared down at the front of her sweater as a noxious odor filled the air.

"What the hell?" Clay shouted. He stared at her for a moment and then grabbed her sweater by one side and ripped it off her. He tossed it to the ground. "Did it get on your blouse? On your skin?" he asked urgently.

"N…no." She stared at him, her head spinning with what had just happened. "What is it? It smells like rotten eggs."

"It's sulfuric acid."

"S…sulfuric…" Her voice trailed away as stunned shock swept through her. She stared at Clay and then looked down at her sweater. The acid had already begun eating away at the cotton threads.

Her knees weakened and the crowd around them

blurred. Acid. As she thought about what would have happened if the liquid had hit her face, a chill she had never felt before iced her entire body.

Clay pulled her close to his side, along with the two children who obviously knew something was horribly wrong. She leaned into him, desperately needing his warmth, his strong support.

"We need to call Dillon," he said and pulled his cell phone from his pocket.

"Sh…should we pick up the sweater?" she asked, her teeth chattering in her head.

"No. Don't touch it," Clay replied and then he connected with Dillon. He told the chief of police what had happened and where they were located and then hung up.

"He should be here in just a few minutes."

He tightened his arm around her, as if knowing she needed his strength, his body heat to pull her back from complete hysteria.

It had to be some sort of a horrid mistake. If it wasn't, then that meant somebody had just tried to hurt her, to disfigure her with acid.

Chapter 4

Dillon arrived on the scene and placed the sweater in an evidence bag. Miranda called her mother to come get the children and take them home with her for the night, and Clay and Miranda were now in his truck following Dillon's police car to the station to fill out a report.

Dillon had questioned a lot of people at the fairgrounds as Clay remained with his arm around Miranda. She had trembled like a frightened dog in a thunderstorm despite his arm around her.

He still couldn't believe this had happened. What kind of a damned fool did something like this? He was still in a state of stunned horror.

He now looked over at Miranda. In the dashboard illumination she was pale as a ghost. Her slender fingers nervously twined and untwined in her lap. He had his heater turned on as the night had grown cool and she was without her sweater, but she continued to shiver as if she couldn't get warm…as if she'd never be warm again.

"How are you doing?" he asked gently.

She released a tremulous sigh. "I'm not sure. I'm still in a state of shock. What I'm trying to figure out is why anybody would have something like that at a carnival?"

Clay clenched the steering wheel a little bit tighter. "I can't imagine why anyone would ever have sulfuric acid anywhere but in a battery. It's not exactly the kind of stuff you just put in a cup and walk around with."

"It had to have been in some kind of an open container. Did you see anyone holding anything strange?" Her voice held a slight tremor.

"To be honest, I wasn't paying attention to the people around us. I was just trying to get through the crowd with all of us together. I'm sorry."

She released a small, humorless laugh. "No need to apologize. Who knew we had to be on the look-out for a crazy acid thrower?"

She shivered once again and Clay reached out and took one of her hands in his. "Dillon will be able to figure it all out," he said with more conviction than he felt. "At least it didn't splash on your skin."

"No, but it ate my favorite white sweater."

He squeezed her hand and then released it as he turned into a parking place in front of the Bitterroot Police Department. Dillon had disappeared around the corner to park in the back of the building.

"Look at it this way, you can always get another white sweater, but you can't get another pretty face," he replied.

He turned off the engine and together they got out of the truck and went through the front door where dispatcher Annie O'Brian greeted them in obvious surprise.

Before they could speak, the door behind Annie's desk opened and Dillon gestured for them to follow him down a hallway. Dillon's private office was Spartan. No interesting pictures on the walls, no official-looking framed documents announcing Dillon's awesomeness. There was just a large desk holding a computer and a framed picture of Cassie. A leather chair was behind the desk with two straight-backed chairs facing it.

Dillon sat at the desk, and Clay and Miranda took the other chairs. As Clay eased down, the tension that had twisted in his guts finally eased a bit. However, it didn't go away altogether. If that acid had hit anywhere else on Miranda it could have caused real harm to her.

"So, tell me again exactly what happened," Dillon said to Miranda. As she told him about being shoved aside and then the liquid being splashed on her, Clay's stomach muscles twisted tight once again.

Had she been pushed aside intentionally in an effort to isolate her from Clay and the children so the acid would only hit her? The thought of the attack being that personal chilled him to the bone.

For him, the evening had only confirmed that he wanted to know more about her and spend more time with her. Being at the carnival with her and her children had made for one of the very best nights of his life…until the end.

He believed tonight he'd seen the real Miranda, with a warm sparkle in her eyes and ready laughter on her lips. But at the moment he was frightened for her.

"And neither of you saw who threw it?" Dillon asked.

"Not me," Clay replied with deep regret.

"I have no idea who threw it on me," Miranda replied. "There were so many people."

"Do you know of any reason anyone would want to do something like this to you?" Dillon asked.

"I can't imagine," she replied, looking utterly bewildered.

Clay was grateful to see some color returning to her cheeks. "What about those bone-headed kids we ran into?"

"What kids?" Dillon asked.

"We ran into Robby Davies, Glen Thompson and Jason Rogers," she said. "They were showing off and being disrespectful. I think they'd imbibed in some liquid courage."

"I told Robby that someday somebody was going to give him a good ass-whooping." A wave of horrifying guilt swept through him. "Oh, God, I hope I'm not responsible for the attack."

"Don't even think that way," Miranda instantly replied. "I can't believe those boys would be responsible for something like this. They can be rowdy and sometimes a little mean, but this, it's just too... too evil."

"I've had a few run-ins with Robby." Dillon's eyes were dark and thoughtful. "But mostly I'm called out to deal with him over a teenage fight. Certainly nothing as serious as this."

"And Hank wasn't real happy to see me with Miranda," Clay added.

"Hank would never do something like this," Miranda said firmly. "He might be the town drunk, but he isn't capable of doing something like this to me."

"And neither of you remember anyone specific being around you when the acid was thrown?" Dillon asked again as a frown cut across his forehead.

Both Miranda and Clay shook their heads. Dammit, he should have been more aware of things... of the people surrounding them. But how could he have anticipated that somebody would throw acid on Miranda? He still found it hard to believe…and horrifying that it had happened at all.

What he wanted to do at this very moment was wrap his arms tightly around her and carry her off someplace where he knew she would be safe.

"Have you had any fights or arguments with any parents at the school?" Dillon's question pulled Clay from his thoughts. "Or maybe a coworker?"

"No, nothing like that." Miranda's cheeks paled once again. "So you think this was a specific attack on me and not just some random thing?"

Dillon's frown deepened. "Right now I'm not sure what to think. I'm sending your sweater to the lab, but it will take a while to get back results. Before we left the carnival grounds I talked to dozens of people, but nobody confessed to seeing anything."

He stood. "I'll question the boys and continue to investigate, but in the meantime the only advice I can give you is that you might watch your back and let me know immediately if anything else disturbing happens."

Miranda was shaken by the lawman's words. Clay could tell by the darkening of her eyes and the way she half-stumbled out of the chair.

He jumped up and grabbed her by the upper arm to steady her. Hell, he was also badly shaken by Dillon's words. He thanked the lawman and led Miranda out of the building and back to his truck.

"I can't believe this is happening," she said breathlessly as he started the engine.

"I still say it was some kind of a crazy random act," he replied in an effort to ease her fear a little. "You are very well liked and respected in this town."

"But what kind of a person does something like this? Who even thinks about throwing acid on another person? It's the worst kind of evil. It's like something out of a horror movie. I can't even imagine that I know anyone capable of it." She wrapped her arms around herself as if suddenly chilled. "I'm sorry. I'm rambling."

"Ramble away. Most women would be completely hysterical by now."

"I've really never been the hysterical type," she replied. "But, I reserve the right to be hysterical if something like this happens again."

"Let's hope it doesn't come to that." God, he didn't even want to think about something like this happening again to her. He pulled up into her driveway.

She stared at her dark house for a long moment and then turned to look at him. "Uh, would you like to come in to visit for a little while? I'm afraid all I can offer you for a drink is either coffee or cherry Kool-Aid."

He knew if the night had ended without incident she probably wouldn't have invited him inside. But she was scared and he was scared for her. "I've always been a sucker for a good cherry Kool-Aid."

She flashed him a quick, stressed smile. They got out of the truck together and walked up the wobbly porch stairs. "You could definitely use some new stairs and railings," he said as she unlocked the front door.

"Hank has promised to fix them for months. He even showed up here last week in the middle of the night to fix them. He was stinking drunk and I sent him home. I'm beginning to think it's about time to hire somebody else to fix them." She opened the front door and ushered him inside.

He entered a small foyer and followed her into the living room. It was a space that befitted his impression of her. The sofa was dark blue and overstuffed, with big floral throw pillows that immediately offered a welcome to sit and visit for a spell. A bookcase held a television as well as movies, games and storybooks.

There was a faint scent of cinnamon in the air, as if something wonderful had recently been baked. The room held the warmth of family and Clay instantly felt at home.

"Do you really want a glass of Kool-Aid or would you rather have a cup of coffee?"

"The first thing I'd like is a tour of your house." He didn't really care about what the rest of the house looked like, but after the night they'd had he wanted to make sure they were the only two people on the premises.

She looked at him in surprise. "Oh, okay." She led him up the stairs and into the first bedroom on the right. It was an explosion of pink...pink bedspread, pink curtains and a fuzzy pink throw rug on the floor.

"It's a great room for a little girl," he said. He walked over to the closet and opened it. "And good closet space." He turned back to face Miranda.

She stared at him and he was dismayed to see fear darkening her eyes once again. "You aren't just interested in seeing my decorating style or the layout of the house."

He released a small sigh. He'd hoped to be smooth enough that she wouldn't know what he was doing, but he'd obviously failed. "You're right. I want to make sure nobody is here who shouldn't be here."

"Thank you," she said in a small voice.

Fifteen minutes later they were seated at the kitchen table with cups of coffee. He had checked every single room in the house and all the closets. He had also been pleased to see that her doors had both good locks and dead bolts. All the windows on the lower level were also equipped with solid new locks.

"You sure know how to give a man an exciting first date," he said.

"It wasn't a date," she protested.

"Oh, that's right. You don't date. Why not?" A

woman like her should love and be loved. She was not only beautiful, she was also bright and had a musical laugh that would make the birds sing in the trees.

"The main reason is that I'm not looking for a relationship. I'm not interested in marrying again so there's really no point in dating." She took a sip of her coffee and eyed him as she set down the cup. "So, why do you date so much? You must know that your nickname around town is Romeo Madison."

He winced. "I can't figure out this dating thing. If I'm Romeo then all I'm doing is looking for my Juliet. How else do you find that special someone if you don't date?"

"According to rumor, you've definitely been cutting a wide swath through the female population," she said dryly.

"It's not like I'm sleeping with every woman in town," he protested. "It's just that I go out with a woman a couple of times and realize she's not the forever one for me, so I stop seeing her."

"Well, I hope you find that special someone," she replied.

"I'm working on it." He certainly wasn't going to tell her that he was working on it right now and trying to figure out how he could get a second date with her.

"It's getting late," she said after a long moment

of awkward silence. "And to be honest, I'm completely exhausted."

It was an obvious dismissal. He drained his coffee cup and stood. "Walk me to the front door?"

She nodded and also got up from the table. Together they walked to the door and once there he turned to face her. "Try not to worry about what happened tonight. I can't help but believe it was a random attack and had nothing to do with you personally."

"I desperately want that to be true."

She looked so small and so achingly vulnerable. Knowing he risked a major rebuff, he followed through on his desire and pulled her into his arms.

She stiffened, and then relaxed against him. She fit as if she belonged in his arms. She was warm and he could feel the thrust of her breasts against his chest.

His sole reason for embracing her was to comfort her, but as he continued to hold her for several long moments a wave of desire swept through him.

She sighed and raised her face to look at him. Her lips parted slightly and he took advantage of the moment and covered them with his own.

So soft and so wonderfully warm, her lips stirred him and heightened the desire that had been sizzling through him all evening long. He touched the tip of her tongue with his and that's when she halted the kiss.

She reared back and he instantly dropped his arms from around her. Her eyes simmered with an emotion he couldn't quite identify. "That shouldn't have happened." She reached up and touched her lips, then dropped her hand to her side. "I shouldn't have allowed that to happen since we aren't even dating."

"Consider it a kiss from a friend," he replied, wanting nothing more than to repeat the kiss. "Can't we be friends, Miranda?"

Those beautiful eyes of hers narrowed slightly. "We'll see. Good night, Clay, and thank you for everything."

"Night, Miranda." He stepped out of her house and walked down the porch steps to his truck. He got inside, but didn't start the engine right away.

He'd tried to keep things light when he'd been inside her house, but there was definitely a darkness brewing inside him when he thought about the acid attack.

He really wanted to believe it had just been a random act by some sicko, but the way she'd described being pushed aside, as if to isolate her from the others, a second before the acid had been thrown whispered otherwise to him.

Dillon had told her to watch her back. Miranda didn't know it, but Clay intended to watch her back, as well. After all, that's what friends were for.

* * *

Damn. Damn! It had been such a bad throw. The acid hadn't hit her face like it was supposed to. The hope had been that it would eat away Miranda's beautiful features. The hope had been that she'd be horribly scarred and become an object of intense pity to everyone in Bitterroot. No man would ever want her and they would all look at her with revulsion.

But the attack tonight had been a complete failure. With the crowd at the carnival it had been a perfect opportunity and an opportunity like tonight probably wouldn't happen again anytime soon. So it was time to think about a Plan B. And in that plan Miranda Silver just had to die.

Miranda pulled herself out of bed after a night of almost no sleep. Each time the old house had grunted or groaned, she'd shot straight up in bed, her heart beating wildly. She'd gotten up several times to check that each door and all the windows remained locked up tight.

And if the worry about somebody being after her wasn't enough, her thoughts had been consumed with being held in Clay's strong arms and the kiss they had shared.

She now sat at the kitchen table with a cup of coffee and thought about that kiss, that damnable kiss that had kept her tossing and turning all night long with a need for…for something more.

Clay Madison definitely knew how to kiss. His mouth had plied hers with heat, and even though his lips had been soft, they had also held a subtle sense of command that had been downright intoxicating. His kiss had definitely made her tingle from the top of her head to the tips of her toes. Drat the man, anyway.

The carnival had been such fun, and a lot of that fun had come from the fact that he was with her and the kids. He was so charming and so easy to be around, but she'd also seen a hard edge to him when the teenage boys had harassed them.

She had a feeling he was a man who took no crap from anyone. He wouldn't start a fight, but he wouldn't walk away from one, either.

There had been something quite appealing in his defending her honor and forcing an apology out of Robby. Of course, the apology hadn't meant anything. Odd, she'd never seen that kind of behavior from the dark-headed boy. It had to have been due to whatever he and his friends had drunk.

Had those three boys gone off somewhere and gotten some acid and thrown it at her in retaliation? Had Robby been so angry at her he'd wanted to scar her for life?

Or was it somebody else? Did somebody else in this town hate her that much and had that person been the attacker? But who? She couldn't imagine anyone would harbor such ill feelings toward her.

Thankfully at that moment her doorbell rang, pulling her from her troubling thoughts. It was her mother with the kids. She directed Henry and Jenny upstairs to pack their bags for their overnight with Hank and then ushered her mother into the kitchen.

When the two were seated at the table Katherine reached across the wood surface and grabbed Miranda's hand. Her blue eyes simmered with loving concern. "I'm so glad you're okay. Thank God that acid didn't get on your skin or in your eyes. How are you feeling this morning?"

"Tired…still a little bit afraid," Miranda admitted. "Sleep was a little difficult last night."

"I can't imagine anyone in this entire town who has an issue with you."

"To be honest, neither can I," Miranda replied. "I racked my brain all night long trying to think of anyone who, for some reason, might have a grudge against me and I couldn't come up with a single person."

"This all has to be some sort of a horrible mistake." Katherine squeezed her hand and then released it and leaned back in her chair. "So, what does Dillon have to say about all this?"

"I haven't heard from him yet this morning, but last night he was going back to the carnival to question more people. In the meantime he told me to watch my back." She fought off a shiver as she spoke those words aloud.

Katherine frowned. "The locks on your doors are good ones?"

Miranda nodded. "Hank saw to that right after the divorce. He wanted to make sure me and the kids were safe and sound."

"At least the man got one thing right," Katherine replied dryly.

"I just can't imagine why somebody would have acid at a carnival, let alone toss it at me."

"Whoever it is, he is a sick, sick person," Katherine replied vehemently.

"I'm sorry about you unexpectedly being saddled with the kids last night," Miranda said in an effort to change the subject.

"You know I didn't mind a bit. All they talked about was how much fun they had at the carnival with you and Clay. They seem quite taken with him." Her mother lifted one perfectly arched eyebrow. "And how do you feel about him?"

Instantly the memory of his kiss leaped into her head and she felt the warmth of a blush sweep into her cheeks. "He's just a friend. There is absolutely, positively nothing romantic between us. You know how I feel about getting involved with another man."

"That's nonsense. You are a beautiful, smart woman who deserves to have a special man in your life. Besides, you're young enough that you could still give me a couple more grandbabies."

"Mom, there aren't going to be any more grand-babies," Miranda protested.

"Never say never and one can always hope." Katherine got up from the table. "And now I'm leaving so I'm not here when your ex-husband shows up. I'm in no mood to play nice with him today."

"You're in no mood to play nice with him on any day," Miranda said with a laugh.

"You have that right," Katherine replied.

Miranda walked her mother to the door and when they reached it she pulled Miranda into an unexpected hug. "Stay safe, my baby girl. Make sure you're keeping your doors locked at all times."

"Don't worry, Mom. I'm going to be just fine," Miranda assured her. "Besides, it's still a possibility that it was just a random act and has nothing to do with me personally."

"I still want you to be careful," Katherine replied. "What would I do without my best friend?"

Miranda smiled. She was so grateful to have Katherine in her life, not just as a mother but also as her best friend.

Fifteen minutes after Katherine left, Hank showed up, his haggard features drawn with worry. "Miranda, I'm so glad you're all right. After I heard what happened to you last night I called Dillon and told him we needed to get some answers as soon as possible."

"I'm sure Dillon will contact me if and when he

has something to tell me." There was no reason for Hank to get involved with this at all. It really didn't have anything to do with him and the last thing she wanted was a drunken Hank haranguing Dillon at all hours of the day and night. "Kids…your dad is here," she called up the stairs.

The two ran down the stairs and within minutes they were gone. Normally she looked forward to having the day to herself, but today the silence pressed around her like a dark shroud.

She thought about going to the community center to see if there was anything there she could help with. She also thought about calling up a fellow teacher to meet her for lunch, but the truth of the matter was she was more than a little bit afraid to venture out of the house.

Was this the way her life was going to be until she had some answers? Would fear rule each and every movement she made? She couldn't be an effective teacher and a great mom if she was scared all the time.

She'd just sat down at the table to grade some papers when her doorbell rang again. She peeked out the peephole to see Clay on the front porch. She opened the door and saw that he had his ball glove in hand.

With the memory of his very hot kiss far too present in her mind, he was one of the last people she wanted to see at this moment. "Good morning." He swept his hat off his head and gave her his beautiful smile. "Is Henry here? I thought maybe we could toss around a ball for a while."

She looked at him in surprise. "The kids are always with Hank on Saturdays."

"Oh, right. I forgot about that." His expression turned more somber. "Have you heard anything from Dillon this morning?"

"No, nothing. What about you?"

"Same."

She didn't want him to come into the house but now that he was here she wasn't sure she wanted him to leave, either. "Uh…would you like to sit and have some lemonade?" She gestured toward one of the two wicker chairs on the porch.

"Sure, I'd like that." He walked to a chair, placed his hat and the ball glove on the porch next to him and sat.

"I'll just go get the lemonade." She turned and went into the kitchen, chiding herself for inviting him to sit a while. She'd spent the entire morning telling herself she needed to keep her distance from him.

However, the minute he had smiled some of her fear had dissipated and a sense of well-being had swept through her. What was up with that?

Surely it wouldn't hurt to visit for a little while and pass some time with him. At least if they were sitting on the front porch nobody driving by could gossip about her having Clay inside the house while her kids were gone at Hank's.

She poured two tall glasses of lemonade and rejoined him on the porch. She handed him the drink and sat in the chair opposite him.

"What's your favorite color?" he asked.

She looked at him in surprise. "That's an odd question to start a conversation."

"I figure if we're going to be good friends, then I need to know some of those kinds of things about you."

He made the word "friends" sound like something slightly sinful and yet his clear blue eyes radiated complete innocence. "Turquoise. And I'm a Libra. My favorite food is anything Italian. There, now you know everything you need to know about me," she replied.

He laughed. "That hardly scratches the surface, but it's a start."

She gazed at him for a long minute. Clad in a navy T-shirt and jeans and with his blond hair shiny and tousled by a slight breeze, he looked like a model for a calendar of hot cowboys. "Why do you even want to be my friend?" she finally asked.

He cocked his head to one side. "Why wouldn't I want to be? You're pretty and you're smart and it's my belief you can never have too many friends."

"You didn't really forget that Henry wouldn't be home today, did you?"

"Okay, you're right. I didn't forget. The truth is

I wanted to check in on you. I was worried about you. You were pretty shaken up last night." Both his warm gaze and his expression of sweet concern caused her heart to flutter.

She couldn't remember the last time a man had worried about her. "I appreciate it, but I'm fine."

"Then have dinner with me tonight at the café."

"Oh, no," she replied quickly.

"Why not? Wouldn't you like to spend some time at the café instead of here in your house all alone?"

She narrowed her eyes and glared at him. "Clay Madison, don't you dare try to manipulate me by using my own fear against me."

He had the grace to look sheepish. "You're right, that was uncool. So, have dinner with me anyway? I know it wouldn't be a date because you don't date. We'd just be two friends enjoying a meal out together."

She had to admit she was torn. She had really been dreading the long hours of the evening without the kids in the house. Dinner at the café was definitely far more appealing. But if people saw them together at the café on a Saturday night, those people would definitely assume they were dating, especially since they'd also been at the carnival together.

Under the circumstances she wasn't sure she cared what other people thought. It was really just important that she and Clay were on the same page, and she'd made it clear to him she wasn't interested in a relationship.

"Come on, Miranda. It's just dinner. You said you like Italian and on Saturday nights the special at the café is always lasagna."

"All right," she finally capitulated. Rumors had never bothered her before, and all that was important was that Clay understood there wasn't going to be any romance between them. Besides, having dinner out sounded far more appealing than sitting in the quiet house all evening.

"Great," he replied. "Why don't I pick you up around six?"

"That would be fine," she agreed. To her surprise he didn't stand up to leave. "So, what is your favorite color?" she asked after a long awkward silence.

"Sky blue," he replied. "I can't imagine a prettier blue than the Oklahoma sky in the spring."

"Did you always want to be a cowboy?" she asked curiously. Clay had a confidence about him, and even at ease he seemed to own and command the space around him. He seemed like a man satisfied with who he was and that only added to his overall attractiveness.

"No way." He laughed. "When I was younger I wanted to be either a professional ball player or a psychiatrist."

"A psychiatrist?" She looked at him in surprise. "Really?"

He nodded. "Really. I wanted to try to understand why people do what they do." His eyes darkened.

"Like why some people believe it's okay to beat their kids, or why would a mother decide to abandon her children." He shrugged and then laughed, although his laughter didn't sound quite genuine. "And then I was introduced to Cass Holiday and I decided the life of a cowboy was right for me."

"I didn't know Cass personally, but I heard lots of stories about her. I was sorry to hear about her death last year."

"Yeah, she could be tough, but she was like a mother to me and all the others at the ranch." He stood abruptly. "I guess I'd better get out of here." He drained the last of his lemonade and handed her the empty glass. "Thanks for the cold drink and I'll see you at six." He offered her his usual charming smile and she watched as he walked toward his truck in the driveway.

Before he could pull away she went back into the house and relocked the door. She stood there for a long moment, thinking about the man who had just left, the man she was going to have dinner with.

The man she'd thought rather vacuous, the cowboy she'd believed had sailed through his life on his good looks and flashing dimples, had displayed a hint of depth…of a darkness inside him. And she was surprised to realize she was eager to explore that depth—strictly as a friend, of course.

Chapter 5

Clay was thrilled and vaguely surprised that Miranda had actually agreed to have dinner with him. Not only was he looking forward to spending more time with her, but he also knew for sure she would be safe as long as she was with him.

He spent the rest of the afternoon going about his chores—and with a bit of grief nagging at him as thoughts of Cass Holiday flittered through his mind.

He'd been scared to death the first time he'd met her. He'd stood beneath her sharp, speculative gaze in the small formal living room of the ranch house and waited for her to toss him back out on the streets.

"You're kind of a scrawny kid," she'd finally said.

"No worries, we're going to fatten you up and make a man out of you...a great man and a good cowboy."

And that was exactly what she had done. He wasn't so sure about the great man part, but she'd taught him how to rope and how to ride. She'd taught him everything he knew about taking care of cattle and horses.

She had been a tough but fair employer and a successful rancher. But she had also been a mentor and a mother figure who had grown to love fiercely the boys she had helped to raise.

There had been many moments since her death that he had missed her terribly. He knew all the men who had been raised by her had those moments as well. She'd been such a huge force in all of their lives.

He knocked off work at five and went to his room in the bunkhouse to shower and clean up. Thoughts of Miranda filled his mind and he was eager for their evening together to begin. He was just about to leave to go pick up Miranda when Dillon called.

"I've got nothing," the chief said, a deep frustration rife in his voice. "I interviewed dozens of people at the carnival, and I followed up with the three boys you told me about and unfortunately I've got nothing to give to you."

The hope Clay had entertained when he'd seen Dillon's number on his phone quickly died. "So, we still don't know if this was some sort of a crazy random act or if somebody specifically attacked Miranda."

"That's correct. I don't have enough information to know the answer to that. I just got off the phone with Miranda and told her the same thing. Hopefully, it was just a random act. Still, I'd love to arrest somebody. Throwing acid on anyone is a serious offense and I don't want that person walking the streets in my town." Once again Dillon's voice was filled with a frustrated anger.

"I guess all we can hope for is that somebody who knows something will come forward," Clay replied.

"I'll keep you informed if I learn anything new."

"Yeah, or hopefully the perp will get drunk at the Watering Hole and confess to somebody who will then tell me," Clay said. "I'll definitely be keeping my ear to the ground."

"That makes two of us," Dillon replied.

The call ended and Clay headed out of the bunkhouse and toward the huge garage where his truck was parked. He was troubled by Dillon's call. He'd hoped that by now the mystery would be solved and the perpetrator would be behind bars.

He couldn't imagine Miranda having any enemies. She was well-liked by everyone, as far as he knew, but maybe there was something he didn't know about her. Still, he was leaning heavily toward the idea that it was a random act by some nutcase.

Bitterroot definitely had more than its share

of nuts, like Leroy Atkinson, who up until a few months ago, had believed space aliens were rocketing off and on his land. Rumor had it his entire house was lined with aluminum foil to keep spacemen rays from getting into him and harming him.

Then there was Raymond Humes and the men who worked for him. They weren't nuts but they were all crazy mean. Even just thinking about the old man who owned the ranch next to the Holiday place stirred a rich anger inside him.

Although things had been relatively calm between the two ranches through the winter, he figured warmer weather would bring out the worst in Humes's men and there would be the usual criminal mischief going on.

In the past those men had ripped down fences, set fires and stolen cattle from the Holiday Ranch. Raymond Humes had hated Cass, and even after her death he wanted to destroy the very legacy she'd built with her ranch and the men who had loved her.

But it was difficult to believe any of those men had attacked Miranda. They would have absolutely no reason to do such a thing.

The Watering Hole was the most popular bar in town with cheap drinks and a huge dance floor. He definitely hoped the perpetrator would have one too many and tell somebody else that he'd thrown the acid at the carnival.

He shoved all these thoughts away when he pulled

into Miranda's driveway. As always, a touch of excitement fluttered in his chest as he thought about spending more time with her. She must like him a little bit to have agreed to have dinner with him this evening and that made him excited to see what might come next between them.

Before he reached her door it opened and she stepped outside. He nearly lost his breath at her loveliness. The waning sunshine painted her features in a golden glow and sparked in her blond hair.

"You look very nice," he said. Black slacks hugged her long legs and a long-sleeved lightweight pink sweater showcased her slender waist and the shapeliness of her breasts.

"Thank you. You don't clean up so bad yourself."

He was glad he'd decided to wear his best jeans and a blue-and-white pinstriped dress shirt.

"Are you hungry?" he asked as they got into his truck.

"Starving," she replied. "I got busy grading papers this afternoon and forgot to eat lunch."

Clay laughed. "I don't know how anyone ever forgets to eat a meal. I'm usually one of the first ones in line when Cookie puts the food out."

"Is he a good cook?"

"He's great, especially given the fact that he cooks for twelve hungry cowboys," Clay replied. "Are you a good cook?"

"I can hold my own. At least, my kids never complain about what I feed them."

"Do you have a specialty?" he asked.

"My kids would tell you my specialty is my homemade mac and cheese, but I think I make a pretty good spaghetti sauce, as well."

"Mac and cheese is one of my all-time favorites, and talking about all this food has really made me hungry," he replied.

It didn't take long for them to drive from her house to the café. The parking lot was nearly filled, attesting to the popularity of the café, especially on the weekends. Despite the crowd they managed to find an empty booth toward the back.

They had just barely gotten settled in when waitress Carlie Martin greeted them. The pretty young blonde handed them each a menu. "Now, what can I start you two off with to drink?"

"An iced tea," Miranda said.

"Make that two," Clay added.

"So, I assume Dillon called you, too," she said once Carlie had moved away from their booth with their food orders.

"He did, but let's make an agreement not to talk about anything negative while we eat." He smiled at her. "I just want us to relax this evening and I don't want to see any worried frowns on your face."

"Sounds good to me," she replied.

And that was how it went. As they waited for their

orders and then as they ate they didn't mention anything about the acid attack.

She told him how much she loved teaching, but
she was also looking forward to summer and spending more time with her own children.

"It's tough sometimes, juggling everything, and
there are times I feel like I give all my attention and
time to other people's children and not enough to
my own. So during the summers it's really important to give my kids lots of quality time with me."

"What do you like to do?" he asked.

"We always spend lots of time at the city swim-
ming pool."

"That sounds like fun." He tried not to envision
her in a bathing suit. "What else?" he asked in a
desperate attempt to banish the visions that were
attempting to form in his brain.

"We take nature walks and play games in the
back yard, and one day we'll probably drive into
Oklahoma City and go to the zoo. Now, tell me
about you. What is it a cowboy does on the Holiday Ranch?"

He told her about his chores and how the men ro-
tated their duties. She asked him questions, letting
him know she was genuinely interested in the information he was giving her. He also told her how
close he was to the other men who had grown up
with him on the ranch, and even though some of
them were no longer working on the ranch and in-

stead had places of their own, the men remained tight and kept in touch with one another.

Throughout the meal occasionally people stopped by their booth to greet them. Several offered their condolences and concern about what had happened at the carnival. Thankfully those interruptions were brief and didn't interfere with the positive tone of their personal conversation.

She told him about her love for her parents and how much she missed her father. "He was the center of my world," she said. "I was definitely a daddy's girl."

"I didn't know him. What did he do?" he asked.

"He was a mail carrier here in town. At the end of each day he would bring home a piece of special mail for me. It was either a card or a note telling me how much he loved me."

"He sounds like he was a wonderful man," Clay replied, enjoying the glimpse she was giving him into her childhood.

"He was, and watching him die was horrible. My mother grieved deep and hard for him, but she managed to keep it together for me."

"You were lucky."

"What about your parents?" she asked. "Do you have any kind of a relationship with them?"

"None. I'm sure you've heard the stories of the lost boys at Cass's." It was a story most people in town knew. After Cass's husband died she lost all of her help at the ranch. Most of the men walked off because they didn't believe Cass had the toughness to run the big spread. Twelve runaway boys who were living on the streets in Oklahoma City were brought in to work for her.

"You know I'm one of those lost boys," he continued. "I ran away from home when I was thirteen. Thank goodness I was only on the streets in Oklahoma City for a couple of months when a social worker who was friends with Cass took me to Cass's ranch to work."

She gazed at him curiously. "Why did you run away? What made you choose living on the streets instead of living with your parents?"

Clay's head filled with the memories of the beatings he'd taken from his father. As bad as the beatings had been, the verbal and emotional abuse had been equally horrible.

You're nothing but a pathetic and ugly kid. You're as ugly as your whore of a mother was. She was so ugly nobody else would have her. I married her 'cause I felt sorry for her. And I feel sorry for you, kid, having to wear that ugly face for the rest of your life.

As his father's voice played in his head, Clay's surroundings melted away. He was no longer in the busy café, but instead was in the small farmhouse where he'd been beaten and abused on a regular basis. Old anger combined with a wealth of remembered pain and whirled around in his head.

A warm touch to the back of his hand on the table pulled him out of his miserable memories. He blinked and Miranda came back into focus, her pretty eyes filled with concern. "Clay, you don't have to talk about any of this if you don't want to."

He flashed her a practiced carefree smile. "No, it's fine. I ran away because my father was a brutal man who beat me almost every day."

"And your mother?"

"Left when I was eight years old." He kept his smile in place even as his heart constricted with the bewilderment and abandonment of a little boy. "She left and I never saw her again."

"Oh, I'm so sorry, Clay."

"All's well that ends well, right? My life might have had a bit of a rough start, but I had a really good life with Cass on the ranch and hope to remain working on the ranch for a long time to come. And now are you ready for some dessert?"

He tried not to tap into those memories of his parents too often because they brought such pain with them. He just wanted to change the subject now and not think about that time of his life anymore.

They lingered over apple pie and coffee. She shared the antics of some of her students, making him laugh, and he in turn told her about the mischief and the bonding of the twelve young men who had come to Cass's ranch as nothing more than kids.

"There was one summer when firecrackers and smoke bombs were popular among us boys," he said. "We'd toss the smoke bombs into a bathroom in one of the bunk rooms when the occupant was…uh… taking care of business. The cowboy would race outside, pulling up his britches and cussing as pink smoke surrounded him."

"That's awful," she said with a laugh.

"It is. We thought it was hilarious, but at the time we were all about fourteen years old. Boys that age think stuff like that is funny. That was about the same time we started sneaking in to Sawyer's room and putting different things into his bed."

"I know Sawyer. Janis is a friend of mine," she replied.

Sawyer Quincy was a fellow cowboy at the ranch and he'd found his forever gal in Janis Little, a pretty woman who worked as a waitress at the Watering Hole.

"Yeah, but I'll bet you didn't know that Sawyer sleeps like a dead person, especially if he's had a few beers, although he's completely quit drinking now."

"So, what kinds of things did you put in his bed?" she asked, her eyes sparkling as if in anticipation of another laugh.

"Tuna, dead fish…stinky cheese," he stopped talking as he looked just past her shoulder and saw a familiar trio of young men approaching their booth. "Brace yourself," he said. "Here comes potential trouble."

Before he could say anything more, Robby, Jason and Glen stopped at the side of their table. "Ms. Silver, we want to talk to you. I know we acted like jerks last night at the carnival," Robby said. "To be honest, we were pretty drunk." His cheeks burned a bright red.

"But we would never do anything to hurt you," Glen blurted out. "We'd never do anything to really hurt anyone."

"Chief Bowie told us what happened to you and I swear we had nothing to do with it," Robby continued. "Somebody throwing acid…that's, like, totally messed up."

"Yeah, and we'd never do anything like that," Jason said.

They all appeared quite earnest and Clay was inclined to believe them, but he also knew how well teenagers could look somebody right in the eye and lie. "I appreciate you stopping by to tell me that," Miranda said.

"If we hadn't seen you here, then we were planning on coming to talk to you before school started on Monday morning. I'll admit we were all drinking a little bit and acted like total idiots, but there's no way we'd do something like what happened to you."

Robby looked at Clay and his cheeks flushed a

pale pink. "And I'm sorry I was disrespectful to you. I was being stupid and trying to look cool, but it wasn't cool."

"Apology accepted," Clay said.

"Then we'll just leave you alone now," Glen said.

"They really aren't bad kids," Miranda said as the three left their booth and instead took a table closer to the front of the café. "I believe they're innocent in what happened." She frowned and raised a hand to her cheek, as if imagining what might have happened had the acid made contact with her skin.

"Hey, hey…no frowning," he said. "We agreed we weren't going to think about this tonight. Besides, frowning and stewing about it won't get us any answers."

"You're right," she said and dropped her hand back to the table. "This has been nice. Thank you, Clay, for getting me out of the house this evening and being such good company."

It had been better than nice for him. He'd waited all evening to get a sign, a familiar bad feeling that she just wasn't the one for him, but tonight had done nothing to put him off. Rather, as the evening was wrapping up he was already looking forward to the next time they'd be together.

A half an hour later they pulled up in the driveway of her house. "No need for you to get out of the truck," she said as she opened the passenger door.

"Nonsense, I always walk a lady to her front door," he replied and got out of the truck.

It was a beautiful evening. The moon was almost full and stars lit the endless night sky. He was so hoping to get another kiss from her.

As they walked up toward her front door, that's all he could think about. Her soft, warm lips would probably taste a little of cinnamon from the piece of apple pie she'd enjoyed. He wanted to taste that…he wanted to taste her mouth once again.

The walkway from where he parked to her front door suddenly seemed to go on forever. He just wanted to reach the door and kiss her.

"Thanks, Clay, for a wonderful evening," she said.

"No problem. I've really enjoyed it. I guess I'll see you Monday afternoon when I come to practice with Henry," he said as she turned to unlock her front door.

"Okay, then I'll see you Monday," she replied without turning back around to face him, and then she was gone…locked inside her house while he stood on her porch with an insatiable hunger that wouldn't be satisfied tonight.

Miranda released a deep sigh as the school bell rang to release the students from another day of school. Mondays were usually tough days, but today had been particularly long and stressful.

She'd tossed and turned most of the night before, still thinking about some acid-throwing madman. When she finally fell asleep, her dreams had been of a tall figure chasing her down a dark street with a large canister of what she knew was acid in his hand.

During her drive to work that morning she'd been half-scared that somebody would do something to her again. She'd been afraid to be in her car, and then she'd been afraid to walk the distance from the staff parking to the school door.

Had she been the specific target of the acid attack? Would that person attack her again? If so, then where and when? How did she go about protecting herself from an attack…an attacker not yet identified?

And if she wasn't worrying about that, she was thinking about Clay and his warm smile and even warmer kiss. She thought about how strong and supportive he'd been through the whole ordeal. He'd shown up to check in on her during the morning hours on Saturday and she suspected he'd invited her to dinner in an effort to make her feel safe.

She had to stop spending time with him. There was no question he was a danger to her. Certainly he wasn't a physical danger, but, oh…he was such a danger to her desire not to get involved with him.

Every little thing she learned about him only whetted her appetite to know a little bit more. The small glimpse she'd had into his childhood had not only half-broken her heart for him but had also made her wonder what kind of internal scars had been left behind.

And wondering was definitely dangerous. To wonder about him implied an interest in him, a desire to know more about him. She didn't want to acknowledge she felt that way.

When he'd brought her home from the café, she intentionally hadn't turned around to tell him goodnight. The setting had been too evocative, with the moon and stars bright overhead and Clay's desire shining from his eyes.

She somehow knew he'd intended to kiss her again and she couldn't allow that to happen. She liked kissing him too much, and besides, friends shouldn't kiss that way. Even thinking about it caused a rivulet of warmth to work through her.

Fellow teacher Paula Durrand stepped into Miranda's classroom. Paula was a petite brunette who taught algebra. She, too, was divorced and had two young children, and the two women had often commiserated with each other about being single parents.

"Hey, are you getting out of here tonight or have you decided to spend the night?" she asked with a grin.

"If I was going to spend the night without my kids and away from my home, this definitely wouldn't be the place I'd choose to stay." Miranda laughed. "I've had more than enough of here for one day."

"Usually you're gone before I leave." Paula perched her trim bottom on the corner of Miranda's desk. "Everything okay with you?"

"As okay as it can be. I just got caught up in my own thoughts and temporarily lost track of time."

"I'm sure you can't help but think about what happened at the carnival on Friday night and I'm sorry you have to even think about that," Paula said sympathetically. "When I heard about it, I was horrified."

"That makes two of us," Miranda replied dryly. "I can't help that it keeps playing over and over again in my mind. I just wish Dillon would figure out who is responsible and get the person behind bars."

"Even if the attack was random, it's appalling that anyone would do something like that here in Bitterroot. You sometimes hear about these things happening in a bigger city but usually it's the work of a crazy spurned lover."

"And I certainly don't have any of those in my life," Miranda replied.

Paula stood. "Get your things together and I'll walk you to your car."

Minutes later the two women exited the high school. It was another beautiful day with the sun shining brightly in a perfect blue sky.

As they walked toward the staff parking lot they

shared complaints about a couple of the students. "I'm tempted to get a cord and tie Bret Samuels to his chair for the duration of the rest of my classes with him. I swear that kid spent most of the class time today wandering around the room and distracting the other students."

"All that would get you is fired," Miranda replied with a laugh. "Just remember, there are only seven more days left. After next Monday we can relax."

"And start preparing for another year of hell." Paula laughed. "You know I'm just venting after a particularly long day. I absolutely love what I do."

"I know that. How are the kids?"

"They're doing okay. Jimmy has decided he wants to be an astronaut and has taken to wearing a helmet all the time, including to bed."

Miranda laughed. "Henry wants to be a cowboy like Clay Madison."

Paula's dark eyes gazed at her curiously. "What's up with the two of you? I know you were with him at the carnival, and rumor has it the two of you were eating at the café on Saturday night."

"We're just friends. It's no big deal," Miranda replied quickly. Instantly her brain filled with the memory of his kiss and heat leaped into her cheeks.

"None of my male friends make me blush like you're doing right now," Paula said with a knowing grin.

"I could never have a romantic relationship with Clay. He's too much like Hank. I know he hangs out at the Watering Hole a lot and everyone knows about his reputation with the women."

"Clay is nothing like your ex-husband," Paula scoffed. "Clay works hard and if he wants to spend his downtime dancing and drinking at the Watering Hole and taking women out on dates, at least he's single. Hank did all of that when he was married to you. Sorry to say it so bluntly, but we both know it's the truth."

They reached Miranda's car. "This is a crazy conversation to be having, because Clay and I are just friends."

"If you say so," Paula replied with an easy laugh.

"I'll see you in the morning, Paula."

"Bright and early. Have a good night." As Paula headed to her own car parked nearby, Miranda slid into hers. She started the engine and glanced at the clock on the dash. Thank goodness Paula had pulled her out of her reverie in the classroom. Henry and Jenny would be getting off their bus and heading for home in fifteen minutes. She'd now have to hurry to beat them home.

They would freak out if they got home and she wasn't there.

She pulled out of the parking lot and onto Main Street. There was only one stoplight in the center of town. Hopefully she'd have the green light and could whiz right on through.

She stepped on the gas and thought about what she was going to fix for dinner. She'd taken chicken breasts out of the freezer that morning. Maybe she'd do chicken parmesan with a side of spaghetti. The kids would like that. They loved anything that included pasta.

What she didn't want to think about was the conversation she'd just had with Paula about Clay. She supposed every person in town assumed she and Clay were dating and that was just another reason for her to keep her distance from him from now on.

Glancing down at her speedometer she realized she was speeding, and a short distance away she could see that the approaching traffic light was red.

She stepped on her brake. The pedal slammed down to the floorboards and did nothing to slow her car. Panic leapt into her throat. She tromped on the brake pedal again.

Horror shot an icy chill through her. Oh, God, she had no brakes. She was going way too fast. Ahead of her a delivery truck pulled into the intersection to make a left turn and in horror she realized she was going to hit it broadside.

"No…no…no!"

Suddenly the delivery truck was right in front of her…so big she could see nothing else. And then she was there, slamming into the side. Pain crashed through her and the world spun dizzily.

Then, thankfully, she fell into the sweet oblivion of darkness.

Chapter 6

There was one chore on the ranch that Clay never minded doing and that was cleaning and polishing the tack. He now worked in a small room in the stable that smelled of rich leather and polish, of horses and hay.

He liked taking something dirty and working on it until it looked all shiny and new again. It somehow soothed his soul and it reminded him of his own life.

He'd arrived at the ranch a dirty kid believing he was ugly and somehow abhorrent to others. Why else would his father beat him? Why else would his mother leave him? He'd arrived here believing that something was very wrong with him.

Big Cass Holiday had taught him to ride a horse and how to be a good ranch hand. More importantly she had given him dignity and a sense of belonging that he'd never had any place else before in his life.

He'd loved Cass like a mother and he'd mourned deeply when she died a little over a year ago. A vicious spring storm had taken her life. Her body was found on the ground between the big house and the cowboy motel. It was believed she was running to warn her "boys" about the approaching tornado when a tree limb had struck her in the head and killed her.

Cass had been the first person to tell Clay he was a handsome boy. At first he'd thought she was being cruel, because all he saw when he looked in the mirror was the ugly boy his father had claimed him to be. But it wasn't long before he started garnering attention from the young females in town and he began to look at himself differently.

There was still one question that plagued him. If he hadn't really been an ugly kid, then why had his mother left him? All his memories of her were of her loving him and then she had simply been gone.

He focused his attention back on the task at hand and tried to empty his mind. But his mind never really emptied, not since the night he'd shared cupcakes with Miranda and her kids. Whenever there was a minute for a thought to enter his mind, it was usually a thought about the beautiful blonde who enticed and excited him.

He was still concerned about her safety. When he'd thought about her driving to work that morning, he'd prayed that she'd get there safely with nothing out of the ordinary happening to her.

"Hey Clay." Flint walked into the stables, a worried look on his face. "I just got a call from Dixie who was walking down Main Street. She told me Miranda just crashed into the side of a delivery truck with her car and it looked pretty serious."

Clay dropped the bottle of polish he'd been holding as his heart pounded against his ribs. "Is Miranda okay?"

"Dixie didn't know, but somebody called for an ambulance and she was loaded up and taken away."

Flint had barely stopped speaking before Clay was moving toward the door as a hot panic sizzled through him. He raced toward the vehicle shed as questions shot through his brain.

She'd hit a delivery truck? How on earth had something like that happened? And how badly had she been hurt? If there was an ambulance involved then she must have been injured. This was all some kind of a terrible nightmare.

What about Jenny and Henry? If Miranda was headed for the hospital, who would be at the house when the two kids came home from school?

As much as he wanted to rush directly to the hospital to see what was going on, he headed for Miranda's home. If the kids came home to an empty house they would probably be scared and that was the last thing he wanted for them.

He drove as fast as he legally could and when he pulled up in her driveway the two children were seated on the front porch. Their worried frowns changed into smiles as they saw him.

"Mr. Clay, Mommy isn't here and she's always here after school," Jenny said. Despite the tentative smile that curved her little lips, her voice held a tremor of worry.

"Do you know where she is?" Henry asked.

"She got held up for a little while and she sent me over here to take you to your grandmother's for a couple of hours," he replied.

He prayed that Katherine was home and available. As much as he didn't want to worry the children, he was desperate to get to the hospital and find out if Miranda had been seriously hurt.

Oh, God, please don't let her be hurt badly, he mentally prayed as he loaded the kids into his truck and headed the few blocks to Katherine's house.

As he drove, the kids told him all about their days at school. He only half-listened to them while thoughts of Miranda were foremost in his mind.

When they reached Katherine's home he told the kids to wait in the truck until he called for them and went up and knocked on the door of the neat ranch house where Miranda's mother lived alone.

Katherine answered the door. "Clay," she said in surprise.

"Katherine, I hate to break this to you so abruptly, but Miranda has been involved in a car accident."

One of Katherine's hands leaped up to her lips as if to stop an outcry. "I'm on my way to the hospital now, but somebody needs to watch the kids," he continued before she could ask any questions... questions to which he had no answers.

"Of course," she finally managed to gasp out. "I'll keep them as long as necessary. Do you know anything more? Do you know how badly she is hurt?"

"I don't know anything other than she was taken to the hospital. The faster I get there, the better."

"Send the children in," she replied, her voice filled with worry.

Clay turned back to the truck and signaled for Jenny and Henry to get out. He looked back at Katherine. "I haven't mentioned any of this to the children. And I promise I'll call you when I know something further."

"Please call as soon as possible," she said. As she greeted the two kids, Clay turned and ran for his truck. He had no idea how long it had been since Miranda's accident, but each and every minute that passed terrified him.

What was happening with her? He needed to see

her. He needed somebody to tell him that she was just fine…maybe a little bumped and bruised, but nothing more serious than that.

Within minutes he screeched into the Bitterroot Hospital parking lot, parked the truck and raced for the emergency room door. When he shot through the waiting room door he saw Dillon was seated on one of the plastic chairs.

"How is she?" he asked and sank down in the chair next to Dillon's. His heart beat so quickly, so loudly, for a moment he feared he wouldn't even be able to hear the lawman.

"I don't know yet. I'm waiting for somebody to give me an update. She was unconscious when she was brought in."

"Unconscious?" Clay stared at Dillon as if the man had suddenly stopped speaking English. "Wa… was she breathing?"

"Yeah, none of her vital signs seemed to worry anyone, but she definitely got banged up." Dillon frowned.

"But you don't know how banged up?" Clay asked and Dillon shook his head.

"So…what happened? I heard she hit a delivery truck." Clay's heart still beat an unnatural, quickened rhythm.

"I talked to a few people who saw it happen. There was a truck attempting to make a left-hand turn at the traffic light on Main and the driver had just pulled into the intersection." Dillon's frown deepened. "According to the witnesses and the truck driver, Miranda didn't even attempt to brake or stop for the red light. She just plowed right into the side of him. And to make matters worse, her airbag didn't deploy."

For several long moments Clay had no words. All he had was a terrifying fear for her condition and questions about the accident. "Did you tow her car?" he finally asked.

Dillon nodded. "I had it towed to the police garage. I want Elliot to go over it with a fine-tooth comb."

"Good, because you know she would never drive into the side of a truck on purpose." If something besides the air bag had malfunctioned, Elliot Truman would find it. He worked as a mechanic at the local car lot, but he also helped out the police department when he was needed. When it came to vehicles, nobody knew more than Elliot.

Still, Clay was far less interested in the car than he was in Miranda's condition. Was she still unconscious? What did that mean? He stood and began to pace. He was unable to sit still while they waited for somebody to tell them about her condition. What was taking so long? Why didn't someone come out and talk to them?

His cell phone rang. It was Katherine. "I couldn't stand it any longer. Do you have any news?"

"I'm at the emergency room with Dillon now. We're waiting for somebody to let us know how she is. How are the kids?"

"A bit confused by the change in their routine, but they're okay. Meanwhile I'm a nervous wreck. My girl has to be okay, she just has to be," Katherine said fervently.

"Trust me, I feel the same way," he replied. "I promise I'll call you as soon as I know something."

He'd just hung up from Katherine when Dr. Wendall Johnson entered the waiting room. "How is she?" Clay asked with his heart pounding so hard he heard its beat in his head.

"She's awake. We x-rayed her from head to toe and thankfully nothing is broken, but she banged up her knees and somehow twisted her ankle pretty badly. My main concern right now is she hit her forehead pretty hard on the steering wheel and now has a concussion. Thankfully the CAT scan showed no bleeding in the brain or skull fracture. She keeps asking about her children."

"Can I see her?" A rivulet of relief washed through him. At least none of her injuries were life-threatening.

"I'd like to ask her some questions," Dillon added.

"I'm not sure how helpful she'll be right now. She's confused and I don't want you stressing her," Dr. Johnson replied.

"I'll be gentle with her," Dillon said.

"We just moved her from the emergency room to room 105. I want to keep her for the night for observation."

As Dillon headed in the direction of the room, Clay made a quick call back to Katherine to update her, then he hurried down the hallway, needing to see Miranda sooner rather than later.

The hospital bed seemed to swallow her whole. She looked so small and pale, the only color on her face a dark purple bruise that stretched across her forehead. She wore a blue flowered hospital gown that made her big, bewildered eyes appear even more blue.

"Where are my children?" she asked as the two men entered the room. They were joined by Dr. Johnson. "Please, somebody tell me where they are."

"They are safe and sound with your mother," Clay replied softly. She sighed and seemed to relax into the mattress as if his words were an enormous relief.

"Miranda, can you tell me what happened?" Dillon asked.

She frowned and then raised a hand to her forehead as if the expression had hurt her. Clay wanted nothing more than to sit next to her and take her hand in his. But right now he didn't want to distract her from Dillon's questions. It was important to find out what had caused the accident.

"I was in a car accident," she replied. "Where are my children?" she repeated.

"They're with your mother," Clay repeated. "You don't need to worry about them right now."

"Do you remember the car accident?" Dillon asked.

She stared at him blankly. "No...no, Dr. Johnson told me I was in an accident." A look of panic swept over her features. "Am I supposed to remember something? Why can't I remember? Did I hurt somebody? Oh, God...is somebody hurt?"

"No, nobody else was hurt in the accident," Dillon hurriedly assured her. "And don't worry about it if you can't remember right now, Miranda. Maybe we can have another talk tomorrow after you rest," Dillon added. "Dr. Johnson, walk me out?"

The minute the two men left the room Miranda asked about her children once again. Clay assumed the repeat of the question had to do with her concussion. He pulled up a chair next to the side of the bed, picked up her hand and cradled it in his own.

"Everything is going to be all right, Miranda," he said softly. "All you have to worry about right now is resting."

"I feel so confused. My head is aching and I feel a little bit nauseous." She moved restlessly against the sheets. "I need to be home. I need to take care of the kids."

He tightened his hands around hers. "You need to stay right here and not worry about anything."

"Clay, I'm afraid." Her eyes beseeched his. "Why am I so afraid?"

"You don't have to be afraid. I'm right here with you and I'm not going anywhere."

"You have a job to go to," she protested weakly.

"Right now my only job is to be here with you."

She held his gaze for a long moment and then drifted off to sleep. While she slept, Clay stepped out into the hallway to make a couple of phone calls. He first called Katherine to see if the kids would be okay with her overnight and then he called Rudy Bailor, the principal at the high school.

He told Rudy what had happened and that Miranda would possibly need a substitute teacher until the end of the school year. Rudy said he'd take care of it and sent his best wishes to Miranda.

His final phone call was to his boss, Cassie. "Cassie, I'd like to take some vacation time starting immediately," he told her.

"Dillon told me what was going on. Are you planning on helping her out?"

"Definitely. She'll probably be released from the hospital tomorrow and she's going to need some help with the kids."

"You know there's no problem with you taking some time off. The other men will cover for you and I'm glad you're planning on jumping in and helping her. Katherine isn't always in good enough physical condition to do much to help out."

"Miranda can count on me," he replied firmly.

He had no idea what Miranda would think about his decision to move in and take care of things, but a woman with bruised knees, a twisted ankle and a concussion wasn't going to change his mind.

He returned to the room where she was still sleeping and sank back into the chair next to her. How had this happened? In no stretch of his imagination did he believe Miranda was a reckless driver. And witnesses had said she hadn't even slowed down before hitting the truck. Why? Why in God's name had this happened?

The deepening purple of the goose egg on her forehead and the paleness of her face constricted his heart. She was going to be in pain for days. If he could, he'd take every ache and pain away from her.

She probably wasn't going to be happy with him staying with her, but she certainly couldn't depend on Hank for anything. She really needed a friend right now, and Clay intended to be the best friend she could ever have.

He must have fallen asleep in the chair because dusk was seeping in through the window curtains when he jerked awake and saw Dillon step into the room.

The lawman gestured him outside. "What's up?" Clay asked when he joined Dillon in the hallway. His stomach clenched tight as he saw the grim expression on Dillon's face.

"Elliot spent the last couple of hours checking things out on Miranda's car. Her brake lines were cut and the airbag was tampered with."

Clay stared at him, a growing horror tightening his chest. "So, the accident wasn't an accident at all. It was a deliberate attempt to hurt Miranda."

Dillon nodded and a muscle knotted in his jaw. "It was attempted murder and that's what the perpetrator will be charged with."

Attempted murder. The words thundered in Clay's head. Who on earth would want to kill Miranda? This all seemed so surreal. It was a freaking nightmare.

"And this puts the acid attack into a whole new light. I think we can now jump to the easy conclusion that the attack wasn't random," Dillon said. "It was specifically directed at Miranda."

Two attacks…two times somebody had tried to harm Miranda. Who in the hell was behind this? And worse, what might happen next? Questions combined with fear and whirled around and around in Clay's head.

"Can you send somebody to sit guard here at her door so I can go to the ranch and pack a couple of bags? I don't want her left alone for a minute and I don't want anyone coming in to visit her since we don't know who might be a bad guy. When she goes home tomorrow, she's not going to be going alone. I had planned on staying with her to help out. Now

I'll be staying with her to make sure nobody has another opportunity to hurt her."

"I'll send Officer Ramirez here to sit guard so you can do what you need to do. Meanwhile I'll be doing everything in my power to get to the bottom of this and see that this perp is behind bars."

Within fifteen minutes Officer Juan Ramirez arrived and settled in a chair outside of Miranda's door. He assured Clay nobody would get into the room.

Clay left the hospital, and as he drove back to the ranch his head continued to whirl with questions that had no answers. Why was this happening and who was behind it?

Thank God she had survived the crash. It could have been so much worse. Just thinking about what might have happened sent a chill up his spine. Without brakes and without an airbag, she could have easily been killed.

In no time he was back at the ranch and in his room, packing a duffel bag full of clothes. Flint and Mac appeared in his doorway. "How's Miranda?" Flint asked.

"Banged up and she has a concussion," Clay replied.

"What are you doing?" Mac asked.

"Packing up to move in with Miranda." He told the two men about the slashed brake lines and that the air bag had been tampered with and hadn't deployed.

"Who would want to hurt her?" Mac asked incredulously.

"That is the twenty-four million dollar question," Clay replied as he pulled a second, smaller duffel bag out from beneath his bed in which to pack some toiletries.

"So this means the acid attack was really directed at Miranda?" Mac asked.

"It would seem so." Even thinking about it made Clay's muscles clench with fight-or-flight adrenaline.

"Man, that's crazy," Mac said.

"Does she know you're planning on moving in with her?" Flint asked.

"No. But I have a feeling when she learns about why she had the accident she won't argue with me about it." Clay frowned and unlocked his top dresser drawer. He took out his holster and gun and then looked at his two friends. "Somebody has tried to hurt her twice now. If anyone tries it a third time and I'm there, I'll shoot to kill."

Miranda blinked against the pain that threatened to splinter her head. She glanced toward the window and was surprised to see morning lighting the horizon.

What day was it? Had she gone to school yesterday? The day before? How many days and nights had she been here? Were her children all right with her mother?

There was a lingering confusion about so many things. She couldn't remember anything about the accident, and right now there was a fog in her brain that refused to lift.

She turned her head in the other direction and was surprised to see Clay slumped down in the nearby chair and sound asleep.

She knew he'd been there throughout the night, although she wasn't sure why. Had it just been one night or a week? She didn't know. Still, she'd been grateful that he was there when she'd awakened and had assured her, time and time again, that her children were fine and she had nothing to worry about.

She stared at him thoughtfully. His hair was tousled and his features at rest were as handsome as when he was awake and animated. Why was he still here? She no longer knew exactly what to think about him. All she knew at the moment was that she was intensely grateful to him for seeing to it that her kids were safe and sound at her mother's house.

As sleep continued to ease away, her body began to protest any other kind of movement. Her knees hurt and her right ankle throbbed with an intense pain. Her head ached and her forehead hurt.

She had no memory of the accident but had been

told about it. Right now she felt as if she hadn't hit the side of a truck but rather had been run over by it.

She suddenly realized Clay's bright blue eyes were open. Slowly a smile curved his lips. "Good morning," he said while straightening up in the chair.

"I'm not so sure it's a good morning," she replied.

Instantly his smile fell away and instead he looked at her with sympathy. "Are you in pain?"

"I think the only place that doesn't hurt on me is my eyeballs," she said with an attempt at laughter.

He didn't laugh in return. His gaze remained soft and sympathetic. "Do you want me to call for a nurse? Maybe they can give you something for your pain."

"No, I don't want to take anything. I just want to know when I can go home. I need to be home and taking care of things there."

"Whoa, slow down. There is absolutely nothing you need to take care of right now. You'll be able to go home when the doctor assures me it's okay. You won't be going home a minute before that."

She continued to eye him. "When did you get appointed the boss?"

He smiled at her. "The minute you managed to get a concussion."

"So, when my concussion gets better, then I get to be the boss?"

He laughed, the rich, deep sound filling the hospital room and momentarily making her feel better. "Yes, you get to be boss once you're back on your feet and well," he agreed.

She frowned, still confused about things. "I need to call somebody to pick me up from here."

"You don't need to call anyone. I'm your ride or die kind of guy. I'll get you home safe and sound. Now, I think I hear the breakfast carts starting to make the rounds. Are you hungry?" he asked.

"Not at all." The very thought of food made her feel nauseous once again.

"You should try to eat something," he urged.

She shook her head and then winced at the pain the movement caused. "Maybe later."

It was just before noon when Dr. Johnson came into the room. After greeting them both, he gazed at Miranda. "How are you feeling today?"

"Stiff and sore, and maybe just a little bit foggy in the brain," she admitted. "But I need to go home. I want to go home."

"The only way I'll allow you to go home is if you stay down, and I do mean down for a week to ten days. You need to rest your brain, so no video games or surfing the web, and definitely no driving. You also should stay off that ankle and elevate it."

She stared at him in dismay. How was she supposed to function with all those limitations? How was she supposed to be a teacher and a mother?

"What about my work?" she finally asked.

"No work for the time being," Dr. Johnson said.

"It's taken care of," Clay replied. "I called Rudy and told him you needed a substitute teacher to finish out the school year."

She frowned at him, unsure if she should be angry at his presumptuousness or grateful that he'd already taken care of it. She suddenly was overwhelmed. "I just really want to go home." She wanted to be at her own house and have her children with her. She didn't know how she was going to manage things, but somehow she'd have to figure it out. She just needed the fog to lift in her brain and for the pain in her head to ease a bit and then she'd be fine.

"Okay, as long as you understand your restrictions, I'll release you," Dr. Johnson said. "I'll send in Katie to help you get dressed. Clay…walk out with me?"

Katie Francis was young with a bright smile. She had been Miranda's student four years prior and had been stellar. When she entered the room, she had a pair of crutches with her.

"Dr. Johnson thought you might need these because of your sprained ankle."

"Oh, I don't think it's that bad," Miranda replied.

It was that bad…and worse. By the time she was dressed and ready to leave, she almost wanted to crawl back into the hospital bed and forget about going home. Her balance was off and her headache had returned big-time. Her ankle was so painful she couldn't put any weight on it and exhaustion tugged at her even though she had done nothing more than get out of bed and get dressed. She had never felt so bad in her life and she fought against tears that threatened to fall.

Clay returned to the room. "All ready to go?" He stepped close to her and grimaced. "You look like you could faint at any moment."

"I'm fine," she replied and tried to force a smile, but she knew it didn't quite make it to her lips. "At least, I'll be fine once I'm home." For the first time she noticed that he wore a gun belt with a gun nestled inside the holster. "Are you expecting a shoot-out on the way out of here?"

"No, but if there is one then I'm fully prepared. You know, it's a Boy Scout kind of thing…always be prepared."

"Clay Madison, you are no Boy Scout," she replied.

Once again he laughed. "Come on, let's get you home."

Katie walked out with them and it didn't take more than two steps for Miranda to realize maneuvering the crutches was a particular form of torture.

Clay must have sensed her discomfort. "Stop," he said before they had even reached the end of the hallway outside of her room. In one smooth movement he took the crutches from her, handed them to Katie and scooped Miranda up in his arms.

She wanted to protest and yet she wanted to lean her head against his broad chest. She was intensely grateful not to be trying to walk with the crutches, but still she stiffened up against him.

"Relax… I've got you," he murmured softly.

She told herself it was nothing more than momentary gratitude that allowed her to relax into him. He didn't really mean anything to her. He was just a physical convenience at this particular time. If he could simply get her home, he could get back to his life and she'd get back to hers. Once again, she fought against uncharacteristic tears.

She wasn't a crier, never had been and hopefully never would be. When Hank had gotten drunk night after night during their marriage she hadn't shed a tear. When she realized he'd been cheating on her, she hadn't cried. So why did she feel like crying now?

She couldn't deny the appeal of Clay's strong arms around her. He smelled like soap and shaving cream and that hint of fresh-smelling cologne that belonged to him alone.

As he carried her out of the hospital, she gave in to her immediate desire and leaned her head against his broad chest. His heart beat strong and steady beneath her ear. She closed her eyes and didn't open them again until she was tucked into the passenger seat of his truck.

As he drove her home, her brain worked to try

to make sense of everything that had happened. "Where's my car?" she asked.

"It needed to be towed."

"I need to call my insurance, but how can I tell them what happened when I don't remember the accident?" Anxiety rose up inside her. How had she managed to run into the side of a truck? Had she been daydreaming? Speeding? "I still don't understand how this all happened."

"I'll help you with the insurance issue. You are not supposed to be thinking about or worrying about anything right now," he replied in a chiding tone. "The doctor said your brain needs to rest."

"I can't help what my brain is doing right now. Thank God the kids weren't in the car with me." She looked at his handsome profile. "Thank you for thinking of my kids and seeing that they were taken care of."

"I figured they might get scared if they got home from school and you weren't there, and the last thing I wanted was for them to be scared."

She stared at him for a long moment and then gazed out the passenger window. Having Clay with her now was every bit as confusing as everything else that had happened to her in the last twenty-four hours.

As they pulled into her driveway, she looked at him once again. "Why are you doing all this, Clay? Why are you helping me?"

He turned off the truck engine and turned to look at her. "Because you need the help and I'm able to help you."

"I'm not going to sleep with you," she said firmly. If nothing else was clear in her head it seemed important that she make that clear to him.

His lips turned up into his devastating smile. "Darlin', I haven't asked you to." He opened his door. "Now, how about you give me your house key and let's get you inside." Thankfully her purse had been brought to her in the hospital.

She pulled out her keys and handed them over. As she tried to get out of the truck he stopped her and then hurried around and scooped her up in his arms once again.

At the front door he somehow managed to maneuver her and open the door at the same time. "Bed or sofa?" he asked as he stepped inside.

"Sofa."

He eased her down and grabbed a throw pillow to put under her ankle. "Do you need a blanket or maybe something to drink?"

"No, thanks. I'm fine. Clay, I really appreciate everything you've done. I'm sure Cassie could use you back at the ranch now."

He sank down into the chair opposite the sofa. "Actually, I'm on vacation for the next couple of weeks. There's no reason why I can't stay here and help you out with the kids until you get better."

She stared at him in surprise. "Stay here? Oh, that's not necessary." The last thing she needed was to have Clay in her house where she'd be able to smell his scent, hear his laughter and see his smile 24/7. She didn't want to be beholden to him any more than she already was. He was a danger to her on an emotional level.

"How are you going to handle everything?" he asked. "Right now you can't even put weight on that ankle and the doctor said you need to stay down for a week to ten days. You can't get up the stairs to your bedroom. How are you going to take care of the kids? The most important thing you need to do is rest your brain. You have a concussion, Miranda."

Once again her eyes burned with unshed tears. "My mom can help out some," she replied.

"You know as well as I do that your mom can't handle everything for any length of time. She has health problems of her own. I've got packed bags in the truck and I'm ready to move in."

"I just don't think that's a good idea."

He held her gaze for a long moment. His eyes appeared to darken in hue and then he released a deep sigh. "Miranda, I didn't want to tell you this until you were feeling a little better, but I guess I have to tell you right now."

The grim expression on his face and an energy that suddenly seemed to waft from him made her heart beat faster and anxiety swell in her chest. "Tell me what?"

"Your car accident wasn't really an accident. Somebody cut your brake line and disabled your air bag. Somebody tried to kill you, Miranda, and I'm not leaving your side until Dillon gets that somebody arrested and behind bars."

She stared at him, and as his words sank in, the tears that had threatened all day exploded out of her.

She'd watched him for days, her heart aching with a need so great it threatened to consume her. She wanted to wrap her arms around him and smell his scent. She needed to brush his hair away from his forehead and gaze into his beautiful blue eyes.

However, she was afraid. She was so afraid of rejection, especially now that he appeared to have a woman in his life. Sooner or later she was going to attempt to step back into his life.

But it wouldn't be today.

Chapter 7

Damn. He hadn't meant to make her cry. He hadn't even wanted to tell her the truth about the accident right now. He would have preferred to tell her when she was feeling better and stronger, but she had to understand why he needed to be here with her.

"Hey, hey, don't cry." He jumped up from the chair, walked over and sat on the edge of the sofa next to her hip.

Tears trekked down her cheeks as soft sobs escaped her. She waved him away and covered her face with her hands. "I never, ever cry," she managed to gasp between sobs.

"I'd say, under the circumstances, you're definitely allowed," he said gently. What he wanted to do more than anything was take her in his arms and hold her close. He'd wanted to do that since the moment he first saw her so small and vulnerable in the hospital bed.

But he didn't do it. It wasn't what she needed right now. Instead he got up and returned to his chair as she quickly gained control of her tears. She swiped her cheeks one last time with an angry brush of her fingers.

"How do you know about the car?" she asked.

He explained to her about it being towed to the police garage where the mechanic had come to those conclusions. When he finished she gazed at him, not with tears in her eyes, but rather with a dark fear.

"I could have not only have been killed in a careening car with no brakes, but I also could have killed somebody else. I just don't understand this. Why…and who is doing this to me? What is happening in my life?" Her gaze went from his face to the gun on his hip. "That's why you're wearing your gun, isn't it?"

He nodded. "I'm not going to let anyone hurt you or the kids. That's why I'm moving in." He leaned forward. "You need somebody here at all times, Miranda…and that somebody is me."

"The guest bedroom is up the stairs and the first room on the left," she finally said after a long pause. She then leaned her head back and closed her eyes.

Clay remained seated for several minutes until he realized she'd fallen asleep. Quietly he got out of the chair and went to retrieve his duffel bags and the crutches. Before going back inside, he looked up and down the block, making sure nothing appeared amiss.

When he came back inside he made sure the front door was securely locked and then went upstairs and into the bedroom where he'd be staying. It was a pleasant room with a double bed covered in a pale blue spread. It didn't take him long to hang his clothes in the closet and put underwear and socks in a drawer in the dresser.

He carried the smaller duffle bag into the bathroom next door with the intention of unloading some things. But it was obvious this was the children's bath. The shower curtain boasted two smiling starfish and there were matching towels. Several large bottles of bubble bath sat on the floor next to the tub.

There was no way Clay was going to leave his razors in here. He carried the duffle back to his room without unpacking anything.

He left the room and went into the other bedrooms to check the locks on the windows. Assured that the locks were all in place, he walked back down the stairs to check all the windows and doors in the living room and kitchen. Finally, confident that nobody could easily get into the house, he eased back down into the chair across from where Miranda slept.

Questions once again began to whirl in his head, making him half dizzy. Who? Who was behind these attacks on her? Unfortunately anyone could have had access to her car with it parked in the school parking lot. Teenage boys might know how to cut a brake line, but so might a lot of other people in town.

Was it possible one of the three boys who had accosted them at the carnival was responsible? Or was there somebody else at the school who had a seething, secret hatred of Miranda? A fellow teacher? Somebody working in maintenance?

He was confident Dillon would be working every angle possible, but that certainly didn't stop Clay's burning curiosity. Was it possible Hank was behind the attacks? Did he want full custody of the children? That scenario rang false. Hank was hardly an involved father, and he and Miranda seemed to share a decent relationship. He couldn't see the man who was drunk most of the time having the capacity to plot and then carry out such actions.

A loud knock sounded on the door, waking Miranda from her sleep. It was too early for Katherine to be bringing the kids. He'd spoken to her on the phone earlier that morning and they had agreed that she would feed the children dinner and then bring them home.

He glanced out the peep hole. Well, think of the

devil. He opened the door to Hank and Lori. "Where is she?" Hank pushed past Clay. Lori followed him, her hands filled with a large casserole dish covered in foil.

Hank stopped in his tracks as he saw Miranda on the sofa. "Jeez, you look awful."

"Hank," Lori said in a chiding tone.

"Well, it's the truth," Hank replied. "Look at that bruise on her forehead."

Miranda raised a hand to her head and winced. "At least it's just a bruise and not a cracked skull."

"Well thank God for that," Hank replied.

"Miranda, I brought you that Mexican taco bake that the kids like so much," Lori said. "All you have to do is warm it up. I hope you'll tell us if there's anything we can do for you. If you need us to keep the kids for a few days then you just have to say the word."

"Thanks, but we've got things covered here," Clay replied. He took the casserole dish from Lori and walked it into the kitchen while Hank asked Miranda questions about the accident.

He found it interesting that Miranda told Hank she didn't remember the accident and so didn't know how it had happened. Even more interesting was that she told him her brakes had failed but didn't tell him that her car had been criminally messed with. Thankfully the two didn't stay long.

"You didn't tell him about the car being tampered with," Clay said when they were gone.

"I know eventually he'll find out about it, but I didn't want to hear him bluster and cuss about Dillon not doing enough. My head aches enough without hearing Hank go ballistic. Still, it was nice of Lori to bring the casserole."

"Speaking of food, what can I get for you to eat? Do you want a little dish of the taco bake?"

She frowned. "I'm still really not hungry."

"Honey, you have to put something in your stomach. Do you have some soup in the kitchen?"

She nodded and then winced. "There's some chicken noodle in there."

"Chicken noodle soup coming right up." Before she could protest again he went into the kitchen. He found the soup in the pantry and a large microwavable soup cup in the cabinet.

Within minutes he'd served her the soup with some saltine crackers on the side and then he sank back down in the chair across from her. "You're worrying," he said. "I can tell by the frown on your face."

She ate a spoonful of the soup then released a deep sigh. "It's just… I'm worried about Jenny and Henry."

"What worries you about them? There's no reason to think they are in any danger."

"That's not what's worrying me." She took another spoonful of the soup and looked back at him. "You aren't exactly known around town for your domestic abilities."

"Are you worried somehow I'll kill the kids?" He chuckled. "Miranda, I'm sure I'll figure it all out." She looked at him dubiously. "Trust me, Miranda, I've got this," he assured her. "I've wrestled steers and roped cattle. How hard can it be to run a household with two kids?"

"I guess I'll just have to wait and see how you handle everything," she replied.

He was pleased that she finished her soup and through the rest of the afternoon she napped off and on. The doctor had sent her home with pain pills, and even though he knew she was in pain, she refused to take anything.

At six o'clock Katherine arrived with the children. They ran to Miranda's side. "Wow, that's an awesome bruise," Jenny exclaimed. "Does it hurt?"

"A little," Miranda replied.

"What happened to your foot?" Henry asked.

"I sprained my ankle and so the doctor wrapped it up. He also gave me crutches so I can walk a little."

"Are you going to be okay?" Henry asked with obvious concern.

Miranda smiled at her son. "Honey, I'm going to be just fine."

"Why don't you two go find something to do in your rooms for a little while so I can have a chat with your mom and Clay," Katherine said. Once the kids were gone, she said, "Oh, honey, you were so lucky that this wasn't worse than it was. Dear God, you could have been killed."

"Don't remind me," Miranda replied ruefully.

"What's Dillon saying about all this?" Katherine asked.

"He's coming over tomorrow to update us on the situation," Clay said. "He wanted to give Miranda a chance to get settled back in here before he came by."

"I hope he has some answers." Katherine looked at Clay. "And you won't let anything else happen to her?"

Clay touched the butt of his gun. "Nobody is going to hurt her again as long as I'm around, and I plan on being around until Dillon makes an arrest."

"I wish I could do more to help," Katherine replied in obvious misery. "You'll call me if you get overwhelmed with the kids or anything else?"

"Yeah, but I can assure you we're going to be just fine," Clay said. "I'm going to take care of things here and there's nothing for you to worry about."

Katherine stayed for another half an hour and then left. "The kids need baths, but before we get started on them, I'd like to take a quick shower." Miranda sat up and swung her legs over the side of the sofa.

"Are you sure that's a good idea?" Clay asked worriedly.

"I think it will make me feel better."

"Do you need me to help with anything?"

"Actually, if you could go upstairs to my bathroom and grab the nightgown and robe that's hanging on the back of the door I would appreciate it. I think for the next couple of nights I'll sleep down here on the sofa. The stairs are fairly daunting to me right now."

"You just tell me what you need from up there and I'll be glad to bring it down for you," he replied.

"Just the gown and the robe will do it for tonight."

She remained seated on the sofa as he ran up the stairs and into her bedroom. The midnight blue nightgown and matching robe were exactly where she'd told him they would be. As he took them off the hook, her scent wafted from them and an unexpected heat of desire filled his belly and flooded through his veins.

He knew it was inappropriate under the circumstances, but he had no control over his longing to have more of her. He couldn't help that, for just a moment, his brain filled with the hot memory of kissing her.

Stop it, an internal voice commanded. Stop thinking about your own desire for her. That isn't what she needs from you right now. Right now she needs your tenderness and caring. Right now she needs you as a friend. Hopefully there would be time to explore his desire for her later.

He carried the clothing back down the stairs and handed it to her. "Now, if you could just pass me my crutches," she replied.

Minutes later she was in the downstairs bathroom. While she showered, Clay went upstairs and into Henry's room where the two kids were playing a video game. "We're supposed to catch the fish," Henry explained.

"Do you like to go fishing?" Clay asked as he sat on the edge of Henry's bed.

"We've never been fishing before, except on this game," Jenny replied.

"Maybe when your mom gets better we can all go fishing in the Holiday Ranch pond. There's a lot of big bass in that pond," Clay said.

"That would be so fun," Jenny said.

"I'd like to catch a big bass," Henry replied. "I'd fight him until I landed him." Henry pretended to reel up a fish.

"Me, too," Jenny said and mimicked her brother's actions.

They talked about fishing for several minutes and then the conversation moved on to summer vacation plans. "I forgot to tell you mom signed me up on a baseball team," Henry said. "I'm going to be on the Bitterroot Buffalos."

"That's great," Clay replied.

"And our first practice game is this Thursday," Henry added.

Thursday? How was Clay going to get Henry to his practice game and still be on guard for Miranda? Before he could fully process the issue, he heard the water stop running and knew Miranda would be getting out of the shower.

He went back downstairs and was seated on the chair in the living room when she came into the room. Her hair was damp and she smelled like a bouquet of flowers. Clad in the midnight blue nightgown and robe, she stirred a renewed burn of inappropriate desire inside him.

How could she pull forth such a longing inside him when she was bruised and battered? Again he told himself he should be ashamed of himself for the desire that momentarily swept through him.

"Feel better?" he asked as she set the crutches aside and eased down on the sofa.

"Maybe a little bit." She smiled wanly.

The kids came running down the stairs and into the room. "Henry caught a big fish," Jenny exclaimed.

"That's wonderful," Miranda said. "And what did you catch?" she asked her daughter.

"I caught an old boot," Jenny replied with a small pout. "Next time I'm gonna catch a big fish."

"Mr. Clay said he's gonna take us all fishing for

real in a pond when you feel better," Henry said. "I'm gonna catch a giant bass for real."

"That sounds like fun, but what I need to know now is who wants to take their bath first?" Miranda asked the children.

"I'll go," Jenny said. She got up from the floor where she'd been sitting. "Mr. Clay, are you going home tonight?"

"No, I'm staying here for a while. Is that okay with you?" he asked.

"It's better than okay," Jenny replied.

"And you're going to take care of us while Mommy is hurt?" Henry asked.

"I'm going to take care of you two and your mommy," he said.

"And that's why you both have to be especially good, so that Mr. Clay will stay and take care of you," Miranda said. "And that means it's time for baths."

Clay looked at Miranda. "I want you to stay on that sofa. Just tell me what the routine is and I can take care of it."

"Baths and pajamas," she replied. "And I'd appreciate it if you'd check the temperature of the water before they get into the tub."

"Got it. Now stretch out and relax and think about nothing," he commanded. He then turned to Jenny. "Come on, little lightning bug. Let's go fill the tub."

"How come you called me a lightning bug?" Jenny asked.

"My mother used to call me that. She'd say I was a lightning bug who lit up her life and I'm sure you light up your mother's life, too."

Immediately his heart squeezed tight and a hint of anger rose up inside him. Yes, his mother had said that to him almost every night and yet she'd left him without even a goodbye. She'd just disappeared from his life, never to be seen or heard from again.

His mother remained on his mind as he got the baths ready, first for Jenny and then for Henry. How did a mother just walk away from her kid? Had he been so bad, so ugly that she'd found him impossible to love?

When the baths were finished, he shoved thoughts of his mother deep inside where he tried to keep them all the time…in a place where they couldn't anger or hurt him.

He played a couple of games of Go Fish with the kids at the coffee table while Miranda looked on from her perch on the sofa. Henry was delighted when he won the first game and Jenny crowed with success when she won the second game.

"Okay, it's bedtime, kiddos," Miranda said before they got a chance to start another game.

"But Mom, we need to give Mr. Clay a chance to win a game," Henry protested.

"There's always tomorrow night, and tomorrow

night I'll beat you both," Clay said and gathered up the cards. "Now, give your mother kisses and I'll tuck you both in."

"I'm sorry I can't tuck you in tonight," Miranda said sadly. "I just can't get up the stairs right now."

"It's okay," Jenny said.

"We'll see how Mr. Clay does it tonight," Henry replied.

He followed Henry into his room first and pulled up the sheet around the little boy. He stroked his hand through Henry's blond hair. "I want you to have nothing but happy dreams."

Henry's eyes drifted closed as Clay continued to stroke his hair. "Good night, sweet boy," Clay said. Then he left the room and headed for Jenny's.

She was already in bed and she cast him a sweet smile as he entered. Like he had done with Henry, he tucked the sheet around her neck. "I want you to have happy dreams," he said.

"Are you going to have happy dreams tonight?" she asked.

"I hope so," he replied.

"And you're going to make us breakfast in the morning?"

"I certainly am. Your mommy needs to rest and so I'm going to be here to take care of you two kids for a while. What do you like for breakfast?"

"Pancakes," she replied. "Henry and I love pancakes."

Clay groaned inwardly. Why couldn't she have said she liked a nice bowl of cereal? He'd never made pancakes in his life, but somehow he'd figure it out.

"Then pancakes it is. Now it's time for you to close your eyes and go to sleep," he said.

"Aren't you going to give me a kiss good-night?" she asked. "Mommy always gives us a good-night kiss."

"Well, I certainly want to do it like Mommy." He leaned forward and kissed her on the cheek. As he did, she wrapped her arms around him to give him a big hug. She released him and smiled. "I'm glad you're here. Good night, Mr. Clay."

"Good night, sweetheart," he replied and left the room.

A sweet warmth flooded through him as he headed back down the stairs. It would be so easy to fall in love with Miranda's kids. They were so loving and seemed to accept him with open arms and open hearts.

He returned to the living room. "I think I'll call it a night, too," Miranda said. She winced as she changed positions. "I'm just hoping I get a good night's sleep."

"You'd probably get a better night's sleep if you took one of those pain pills Dr. Johnson sent home with you," Clay replied. He hated that she hurt. He'd seen her discomfort all evening and wished he could take the pain away from her.

"I hate to take a pill. What if one of the kids calls out in the night and I don't hear them?"

"I'll hear them," he assured her. "You've had a long day, Miranda. Now, will you stop being so stubborn and just take a pill?"

"Okay," she finally relented.

He got the pill and a glass of water from the kitchen and then brought them to her. She swallowed the painkiller and he took the glass from her. "What else can I do for you?"

"Would you mind getting me the blanket that's on the top shelf in the hall closet?"

He carried the glass back into the kitchen, then retrieved the soft pink blanket from the closet and carried it to her. He unfolded it and covered her.

"Anything else?" he asked.

"No, thanks. I should be good for the night."

"Before you go to sleep you need to tell me about the morning routine with the kids."

As she told him about breakfast and bus times, all he could think about was his desire to curl up next to her on the sofa beneath the fuzzy, soft blanket and hold her through the night.

"You won't bother me if you want to stay up and watch television," she said drowsily.

"Are you sure?"

"Trust me, nothing short of a bomb going off is going to keep me awake tonight." She closed her eyes.

He picked up the remote from the coffee table and turned on the television. He lowered the volume so that it was barely discernable and then sat in the chair.

He didn't really want to watch TV, but he wasn't ready to call it a night. He needed a little time to process everything that had happened and how this time with her was going to work.

He also needed a little time to just stare at her face and thank God that she hadn't been hurt even worse. His stomach muscles clenched tight as he thought of what might have happened.

The attacks on her seemed particularly evil. Who in this town was capable of such madness? Most of the folks in Bitterroot were good people...hardworking and God-fearing. Who was hiding this kind of hatred for Miranda? He couldn't imagine it was somebody he knew.

He remained in the chair for about forty-five minutes and then decided it was time for him to get some shut-eye. Miranda was sleeping peacefully as he stood and turned off the television.

The only thing that made him a little uncomfortable was that she was sleeping down here while he would be in a bedroom upstairs.

He went into the kitchen and grabbed a chair from the table. He then carried it to the front door and wedged it beneath the doorknob. At least with the chair serving as an additional barrier, he'd hear if anyone tried to burst in. In any case, he intended to sleep with one eye open so that he would hear trouble if it decided to make a visit.

He did the same thing with the back door although he didn't really think the perp would be so bold as to try to break in, especially with his truck in the driveway…a definite indication that she wasn't in the house alone with her children.

He turned off the lights, then went upstairs and into the bedroom where he'd be staying while he was here.

He took off his holster and placed his gun on the nightstand where it would be in easy reach should he need it. He stripped to his boxers and got into bed.

Staying here was going to be difficult for him. He was here as a helper and a defender, not as a lover. Still, he couldn't help the way his heart beat a little quicker each time he looked at her.

He had no control over the desire that seemed to jump to life when he got close to her, when he smelled that floral scent that wafted from her. He wanted to kiss her lips, caress her soft skin, and that desire had definitely been an unwelcome guest inside him throughout the afternoon and evening.

But each time it rose up inside of him, he had to tamp it down. She really did need a friend right now and he was determined to be here for her for as long as she needed.

He closed his eyes, seeking sleep, but instead of

falling into pleasant dreams, a frightening thought that had tried to intrude all day sprang fully formed into his head.

There had been two failed attempts to severely hurt or kill Miranda. Whoever was behind those attempts had been thwarted so far.

But he knew in his gut that the person wasn't finished yet. He or she hadn't achieved the ultimate goal. The person would try again. What kept Clay awake for a long time was wondering how and when another attack would happen.

Miranda lay on the sofa and listened to Clay cleaning up the breakfast dishes. This was the third morning that he'd fixed breakfast for the children, checked that they were dressed appropriately and then sent them out the door for the bus stop and school.

If Clay Madison had scared her before with his charm and sexy appeal, he scared her even more now. In the past three days she'd seen yet another side to him.

He'd surprised her with his domesticity. He seemed as comfortable in the kitchen as she guessed he was at the Watering Hole. As the three ate breakfast together each day there was plenty of laughter drifting out of the kitchen.

In the evenings he made dinner and she joined them. With the four of them seated at the table and the children laughing at Clay's bad jokes and silly antics, her heart expanded with remembered dreams.

When the kids had first been born, she'd envisioned this kind of life…her family gathered around a dinner table, sharing the events of their day and laughing together.

But by the time Jenny was born, Hank had already started drinking heavily and more nights than not by dinnertime he was passed out in the bedroom. She'd definitely wanted the fairy tale, but it had been shattered with Hank.

It scared her that she saw whispers of that fairy tale coming back to life with Clay here in her house. Her head told her it was just an illusion and not to be trusted, but her heart wondered if perhaps she had badly misjudged the handsome cowboy. Or was it simple gratitude that had her softening so much toward Clay?

Nobody else in her life would have stepped up to do what he was doing for her now. Nobody else would have put their own life on hold the way he had done for her.

During the past three days the fog in her head from the accident had begun to let up, but her confusion about Clay had only deepened. Was he the party boy Romeo the town had painted him, or was he something else entirely?

She certainly wasn't interested in a romantic relationship with him, but she was curious about him…

about the depths of him and what made him tick. She told herself that getting to know him better would help her pass the time until she got back on her feet.

"Dishes all done," he said as he walked into the living room and sank down onto the chair opposite her. He smiled. "The bruise on your forehead is turning an interesting shade of pale yellow."

"I saw that this morning. I'm hoping in another week or so it will be gone completely. At least I'm starting to feel better."

"I'm glad. It hurt me to see you in so much pain."

Was he just that practiced at saying nice things? Certainly his soft expression as he gazed at her made her want to believe there were genuine feelings behind what he said.

"Can I get you anything?" he asked. "Another cup of coffee or a glass of juice?"

"No, I'm fine. All I want is a little conversation. I feel like for the last couple of days I've done nothing but sleep my life away."

"You needed the rest. Now, conversation I can do," he replied. "What would you like to talk about?"

Before she could respond, there was a knock at the door. Clay jumped out of the chair, his hand on the butt of his gun, opened the door and visibly relaxed as Dillon walked in.

"Good morning," Dillon said. "I figured it was about time for me to update you on what I've been doing."

"Please, sit," Miranda said. She sat up so that Clay could sit on the sofa next to her.

"Would you like a cup of coffee?" Clay asked.

Dillon hesitated a moment and then nodded his head. "A cup of coffee would be great. I only got down one cup this morning before I left the house." He sat in the chair Clay had vacated. "How are you feeling?" he asked as Clay disappeared into the kitchen.

"Better every day, but I still have no memory of the accident," Miranda replied.

"Don't stress about it. Even if you remembered it, your memory probably wouldn't help in the investigation. Thanks," he said to Clay as he returned to the room and handed Dillon a cup of brew.

"So, what's new in the investigation?" Clay asked as he sat next to Miranda.

Dillon released a deep sigh. "I've interviewed most of the staff at the school to see if anyone there knows anything about somebody who might have an issue with you."

"And?" Clay leaned forward.

"And nothing." Dillon took a sip of his coffee and continued. "Everyone I spoke to at the school praised Miranda for being a great coworker and teacher. Nobody had any idea why somebody would be after you."

"I still don't have a clue who might be behind the attacks," Miranda said. She felt as if she was in a horrible nightmare and she couldn't wake up. She didn't even recognize her life right now. "I've thought and thought about it, but nobody comes to mind."

"I have to admit the investigation is at a standstill at the moment," Dillon replied with a deep frown. "Part of the problem is the car was obviously tampered with in the school parking lot. That means it could be any student or teacher who attends the high school or somebody just walking onto the lot off the street. There's no kind of security there."

"So the pool of suspects is huge," Clay said.

"Exactly." Dillon took another drink of coffee. "It's the same with the carnival," he continued. "Half the town was there when you were attacked. I'm hoping somebody will eventually show their hand, but until that happens, I don't know where to take this investigation."

"What about the car? Could you pull any prints off the brake line or the airbag?" Clay asked.

"None. Whoever tampered with it apparently wore gloves," Dillon replied.

Miranda frowned and looked thoughtfully at Clay. "Maybe we've all been looking at this from the wrong angle."

"What do you mean?" Dillon asked.

Miranda looked at Clay once again and then back at Dillon. "Maybe it isn't about somebody from my life. Maybe it's about somebody from Clay's."

"Why would anyone in my life want to hurt you?" Clay asked in obvious bewilderment.

"Maybe it's one of the women you dated who doesn't realize you and I are just friends and she now sees me as a rival," she said. There could be all kinds of women who might not like the fact that she was occupying all of Clay's time.

"I can't imagine anyone I've ever dated going after Miranda," Clay said. "None of them would feel that way about me."

"I figured if there was anyone who might have an issue with you, you would have told me already." Dillon set his cup on the coffee table and withdrew a small pad and pen from his pocket. "Maybe I should take down the names of the women you've dated in the last six months or so."

Clay looked at her and then gazed at Dillon. Miranda was surprised to see the dusty color of a blush filling his cheeks. "Tanya Baker, Christi Landon, Mary Jo Atkins, Kelli Carson and Bonnie Abrahams, but they've all moved on, like I have."

The information fell from his mouth in a rush, as if this was the last thing he wanted to speak about. As he talked to Dillon about each of the women he had dated, it only reminded Miranda of why she didn't want to get involved with him in any romantic way.

"I only dated each of them a couple of times," Clay continued to explain. "And when I stopped seeing them, each one of them were cool with the decision to go our own way. It was all pretty casual. I just can't imagine any one of them being behind the attacks on Miranda. Things weren't that passionate or deep with those women."

"Still, it wouldn't hurt for me to talk to each of them," Dillon replied. He stood. "I'll get back to you if anything breaks, and thanks for the coffee."

"No problem." Clay stood, as well. "I'll walk you out."

He probably wanted to tell Dillon more information about his relationships with those women, Miranda thought. Not that she cared. Not that she cared one little bit.

Clay returned and sank down in the chair facing her. "I dated them, but I didn't sleep with any of them."

"It's really none of my business," she replied.

"But it's important to me that you know I didn't jump into bed with any of them. I don't do that."

"Duly noted," she replied.

They fell into an awkward silence. "Henry has his practice ball game tonight. I need to figure out how to handle it," he finally said.

"What do you mean?" She looked at him curiously. "What's to handle?"

"I need to be in two places at one time. I have to take Henry to the ball field and I need to be here with you."

"There's nothing to handle. I planned on going to the ball game tonight. I want to go."

He frowned. "Are you sure you're up to it?"

"My ankle is a lot better and my brain won't over-work itself watching a ball game. I want to be there and he'll want me to be there." There was no way she was going to miss her son's very first baseball game. Surely it wouldn't be dangerous for her to go as long as Clay was by her side.

"Okay, then we'll all go."

Before either of them could say anything else the doorbell rang once again. This time it was Mary and Halena, who wore a feathered purple hat and car-ried a casserole dish. "We brought food," she said and handed the dish to Clay. "It's a chicken and corn casserole with some of my special seasoning. When you eat it, you will be so happy you'll start wear-ing hats." Both Miranda and Clay laughed as Mary rolled her eyes.

"We just wanted to see how you were doing," Mary said. "We've been so worried about you since we heard about the accident."

"I'm doing much better than I was a couple of days ago," Miranda replied.

"That's a nasty bruise on your forehead. A hat would hide it," Halena said as she sat in the chair op-posite Miranda. "Maybe when I go home I'll make you one."

Miranda gestured for Mary to sit next to her on

the sofa and Halena sat in the chair. Clay disappeared into the kitchen, leaving them all to visit.

They stayed for almost an hour and after they left Mandy Booth arrived bearing four big cupcakes from her shop.

It was a day for people stopping by to check on her, and before she knew it, the kids were home from school. They ate Halena's chicken casserole for dinner. The woman might be a unique character, but she definitely knew how to cook. The casserole was delicious and by the time Clay cleaned up the kitchen it was time for Henry's baseball game.

"I'm going to remember everything you taught me, Mr. Clay," Henry said once they were in the car and headed to the ball field.

"That's good, but now it's important that you listen to your coach," Clay replied.

"Is Dad coming?" Jenny asked.

"I don't know. I told him about it," Miranda said. She doubted very seriously that Hank would show up, but it would be nice if he did.

Despite the fact that she knew about all the women Clay had dated in the last six months and despite the fact she told herself she had no romantic interest in him, she couldn't help the butterflies that took flight in her stomach when she looked at him.

He looked so darned handsome in his jeans and a light blue T-shirt that displayed firm biceps and his muscled chest. His slightly shaggy hair made her fingers want to dance in the blond strands. His scent filled the interior of the truck and pulled forth a yearning inside her.

And suddenly she was thinking about their kiss. She was immersed in memories of how his lips had warmed her from head to toe and how his strong body had felt against hers. It had been a brief kiss and she hated that it had left her wanting more.

Maybe her concussion had really addled her brains. Surely that was the only reason that during the past three days she'd found herself longing to be in his arms, longing for his lips to once again be on hers.

It had to be gratitude that she was feeling. He had kept things running smoothly at the house with the children and that alone made her more than grateful for his presence. He had stood by and helped the kids with their homework and hadn't blinked an eye when they got out their messy finger paints to make him a picture.

There had been a few times in the mornings before the kids had come down for breakfast that she'd heard him muttering curses right before the garbage disposal ran. She suspected he'd had a few issues with cooking breakfast. But he didn't mention it and neither did she. Secretly she found the whole thing charmingly amusing.

Thankfully they arrived at the ball field and her only thoughts were for her son, who was clad in a red T-shirt with the team's name emblazoned across the front.

There was no kiss from her son as he left their sides and raced toward his team members on the other side of the ball field. Miranda's heart squeezed.

Her little boy was growing up so fast. Today a baseball game...tomorrow driving a car and then getting married. She inwardly laughed at her maudlin silliness but sobered as she thought of the very real possibility that somebody would kill her and she wouldn't be here to see her children grow.

She couldn't imagine it...she didn't want to imagine her children being raised by Hank. She didn't want to imagine her not being here to teach them to drive, to see them off to their first proms, to kiss them good-night each and every night.

How could somebody want to take that all away from her? Who would be heartless enough to leave her children motherless? Was it somebody she saw in school every day? Was it a fellow teacher? Maybe somebody she ate lunch with every day? Or shared hall monitor duties with?

As they settled on the wooden bleachers, she couldn't help but feel the tension that radiated off Clay. His eyes seemed to shoot in all directions and a new energy wafted from him.

She realized he was on duty as her defender, eyeing everyone around them with suspicion. She couldn't help the gratefulness that filled her once again. For the first time since the acid attack, she acknowledged to herself that she was scared.

She was scared because she knew another attack was coming. She just didn't know when or from where it would come.

Chapter 8

They were all still cheering when they returned to the house. Henry's team had won the game 5–3 and Henry had been responsible for two base hits and a spectacular catch that had ended the game in success.

They celebrated by eating the cupcakes Mandy had brought and then, before Clay knew it, it was bath and bedtime for the kids.

Sitting next to Miranda and Jenny on the bleachers and cheering for Henry, feeling like part of a unit instead of a single man, had felt so good. It was what he craved at this time in his life. He'd always wanted a real family to fill the spaces of loneliness and heartache that his mother's absence had left behind.

They said familiarity bred contempt, but he'd been in close quarters with Miranda for days now and there wasn't even a hint of contempt in his heart. The exact opposite was true.

She charmed him with her smiles. Her laughter made his heart feel lighter. Her love for her children awed him. And he had a wealth of desire for her.

He'd learned she wasn't a morning person, that she liked her coffee with cream and no sugar. He also had discovered that when she got overtired she got a little crabby, but he simply considered that part of her charm. Yes, Miranda was definitely getting under his skin like no other woman had before.

Unfortunately, she seemed stuck in the friendship zone where he was concerned and had given him absolutely no indication that she wanted anything more from him.

He now went into the living room where she was seated on the sofa. On all the other evenings he'd been here she'd gone to sleep almost immediately after the kids were tucked in, but tonight she didn't appear to be in a big hurry.

"Tired?" he asked.

"Actually, I think cheering for Henry gave me a second wind." She patted the sofa next to her. "Why don't you sit and entertain me for a little while."

"Entertain you? Are you expecting me to juggle oranges or maybe dance on the coffee table?"

She smiled at him, the first real, warm smile he'd seen from her in days. Instantly an explosion of heat swept through him. "I was actually thinking maybe you could tell me some more funny stories about you and your friends at the ranch, but if you want to dance on the coffee table, I will be a rapt audience of one," she said.

He sank down next to her on the sofa. "Do you like to dance?"

"I used to love it, but I haven't danced in years," she replied.

"Maybe when you're back on your feet we can go dancing at the Watering Hole." The vision of holding her close and moving to a ballad warmed him once again.

"Maybe," she replied. "Now, entertain me with some stories."

For the next half an hour he told her more about the antics of the young runaway men who had found their home at Cass's ranch. A couple of his stories included Adam Benson, the man who had become ranch foreman and had been discovered to be a serial killer.

"You must have been shocked when you found out about Adam," she said.

He nodded. "Almost as shocked as I was when I

found out I wasn't so ugly that I'd scare young children who happened to look at me."

"Why on earth would you ever think that?" She gazed at him with open curiosity and a hint of astonishment.

Clay fought against a swell of emotion that suddenly rose up inside him. He'd never talked about this before. He'd never shared it with any of the other men at the ranch or anyone he'd ever dated. It was at the very core of who he was…a piece of himself he'd never given away.

However, he suddenly wanted to share it with her now. For the first time in his life he felt safe baring his deepest secrets with another person. He realized it might give her a better understanding about who he was and where he'd been.

"From the time I can remember, my dad told me I was ugly. When anyone would look at me, he'd whisper in my ear that they were staring at me because I was so ugly. He told me when my mother left that she left me because she couldn't love me because I was so damned ugly and those words hurt more than any physical beating he ever gave me."

Memories cascaded through his head, bad memories that he knew would always be with him. His childhood had left scars, not only on his heart, but also on his very soul.

"Oh Clay, I'm so sorry," she said softly. She reached out and touched his arm.

"Thanks. You know, people don't realize the power of their words. Trust me, words can hurt far more than fists. I grew up believing I was the ugliest kid on the planet, that even my own parents couldn't love me."

"No wonder you wanted to run away." She withdrew her hand from him, but her eyes continued to be filled with compassion.

"I was about nine when my dad took me to my first carnival. At that time they had a tent of human abnormalities. You know the kind…there was a little person and a woman eight feet tall. There were people with horrible birth defects, and I figured if I did run away, then I would find a carnival and could be the ugliest kid on earth." The emotion he'd tried so hard to contain made his voice crack. He quickly cleared his throat.

"I… I don't even know what to say," she said softly. "Saying I'm sorry for you just seems too inadequate. Was it that way when your mother was there?"

"Yeah, he'd say hateful things, but then at night she would come to tuck me in and would tell me I was her handsome little man and I shouldn't take to heart the things he said to me. But then she left me. She was my only source of softness, of love, and she just walked away."

He stared at her as a hollow wind blew through him. He hadn't been able to understand why his mother had left him when he'd been eight, and he didn't understand it now that he was thirty-three years old. It was a question that would haunt him for the rest of his life.

"Was your father abusive to her?"

"I never saw him hit her, but there were mornings when she had black eyes or a swollen lip and bruises on her arms and legs. It didn't take a rocket scientist for me to figure out something bad was happening between them when I was asleep."

Once again emotion tightened in his chest, almost making it impossible for him to draw a breath. "I wanted to protect her, but he was so big and mean, and the one time I decided to say something to him I got so scared I wet my pants."

Once again she placed her hand on his arm. "And you never heard from your mother again?"

He shook his head. "It was such a sudden and complete abandonment by the most important person in my world. I swore then that I would never be abandoned again, that I would never love anyone that deeply again."

To his horror, tears pressed hot at his eyes and he gazed at her with blurred vision and a sense of helplessness. It was a wounded child in control of him, a lost little boy who had never been allowed to be in control before.

She pulled him into her arms. He leaned into her as the tears burned even hotter. He was appalled.

He was embarrassed, and he was humiliated by his sudden emotional weakness. To that end, he tried to pull away from her, but she held tight and he finally gave in to the embrace…to her warmth and to her comfort.

He didn't allow himself the release of deep sobs and racing tears, rather his tears oozed from his eyes silently. "You didn't deserve the childhood you had," Miranda said softly as she continued to hug him close. "You didn't deserve any of it. Your father should have been put in jail for the way he treated a little boy."

The words soothed him, as did her hands, which moved up and down his back. It was as if she had found that wounded little boy inside him and was loving him like nobody else ever had.

But any vestiges of that little boy slowly faded away as he became aware of the softness of her breasts against his chest. Her evocative scent surrounded him and desire buoyed up inside him to replace his pain.

He raised his head and for a long moment their gazes remained locked. In the depths of her sharp blue eyes he saw compassion…sympathy, but he also saw something else: a simmering emotion he believed he recognized.

Her lips were so close to his and all he could think about was tasting them once again. She parted her lips as if in anticipation and he covered her mouth with his.

Sweet heat rushed through him. She didn't pull away, but rather leaned into him and opened her mouth to allow him deeper entry. His tongue touched her lower lip and then slid in to dance with hers.

Her heart beat a rapid tattoo against his own and he was instantly aroused. His hands tangled in the silk of her hair as he leaned closer…closer still to her. Despite her wearing a bra and a blouse, he thought he felt her nipples harden.

He wanted her. Lordy, he wanted her so badly and he believed she wanted him, too. He tasted desire in her kiss and that had nothing to do with mere friendship.

Their kiss went on forever. Even when they both were half breathless, the kiss continued. He couldn't get enough of her sweet lips beneath his. The fact that she didn't break the kiss or push him away gave him courage.

He slid his hands up beneath her blouse. The skin on her back was so warm and soft and inviting. He wanted to scoop her up in his arms and carry her up to the bed where he'd been sleeping and dreaming about her. Visions of her naked and eager in his arms taunted him. He started to move his hands around to cup her breasts.

"Clay, stop!"

He sprang back from her as if she were on fire.

She stared just past his shoulder to the window and raised a trembling hand to point. "I… I just saw a face. At the window. Somebody is out there." Her voice shook with obvious fear.

Jumping up off the sofa, a new and different kind of adrenaline shot through him. Thank God he hadn't put the chair under the doorknob yet. He unlocked the door and yanked it open. He ran outside where it took a moment for his eyes to adjust to the darkness of night. When they did, he saw a dark figure running up the sidewalk.

Clay took off after him and he could tell it was a him by the size and shape of the person. He ran as fast as he could, his heart nearly exploding out of his chest with his exertions.

The figure veered off the sidewalk and headed for the shadowed blackness between two houses. The last thing Clay wanted to do was to lose sight of the person. He needed to know who had been peeping into Miranda's window and why. Dammit, he needed to catch him.

The runner was fast, but Clay was determined and quickly gained on him. He ignored the stitch in his side and the burn of his calves.

When he was close enough, he lunged forward onto the person's shoulders. The two went down to the ground and rolled. Clay scrambled to his feet and pulled his gun as he stared into Robby Davies's eyes.

"Don't shoot!" Robby curled up into a fetal ball in the grass. "Please…please don't shoot me."

"Get up," Clay commanded.

"I didn't do anything," Robby replied. "You shouldn't pull a gun on me just because I was walking down the sidewalk."

"You weren't just walking…you were running away from Miranda's house. Now, get the hell up before I decide to put a bullet in your leg."

Robby got to his feet. "I didn't do anything wrong," he said again as Clay gestured for him to walk back to Miranda's house.

"You can tell it to Dillon," Clay said. He didn't know what made him angrier: Robby window peeping or that by doing so the kid had ruined Clay's magical moments with Miranda.

Robby refused to speak or look at her while they waited for Dillon to arrive. What had he been doing lurking in the dark of night around her house? Had he been looking for a way to break in? Hoping for a time when she'd be home all alone?

She gazed at the teenager she saw every day in the school hallways. His dark hair looked greasy and unkempt, and his expression was sullen as he stared down at the floor. She had never done anything to make him mad at her, angry enough to try to kill her.

Was he the one who had thrown the acid on her? Cut her brake lines? He'd been at the carnival that night and he had access to her car. And why had he been outside her house and peeping in her window?

Clay also remained silent as they waited for the chief of police to arrive. His grim expression and the energy that wafted from him twisted her stomach in knots of anxiety. She knew Clay was thinking the same thing she was, that Robby might be responsible for trying to kill her twice.

Thank God Clay had managed to catch him. Otherwise they wouldn't have known who had been outside her window. At least now they had somebody as a suspect.

She released a deep sigh of relief when Dillon finally arrived. Clay quickly filled him in and the lawman eyed Robby with obvious suspicion. "What were you doing outside Miranda's house?" he asked.

"I wasn't doing nothing," Robby replied, his gaze still on the floor in front of him.

"You were looking in my window. I saw you, Robby," Miranda replied.

"I didn't mean any harm." Robby's cheeks flushed with color and he finally looked up at Dillon. "Can I talk to you, like, in private?"

Dillon hesitated and then nodded. "Okay, we can step outside, but don't even think about running off because no matter where you run, I'll find you."

"I'm not gonna run off," Robby said.

With a nod to Miranda and Clay, Dillon ushered

Robby outside. "I wonder what excuse he's giving Dillon for being here," she said.

"Who knows, but he has no business being anywhere around your house," Clay replied. "Makes me wonder…" His voice trailed off.

"Makes me wonder, too. Did you see anyone with him?" she asked worriedly.

"No, just him." He frowned. "Unless somebody else ran around the back of the house while I was chasing him. Dillon will find out the truth about who was outside and why."

Was it possible a handful of high school kids were after her? Was it the result of some sort of a sick bet? Was there something going on at the school that she…that nobody knew about? The idea positively terrified her.

Clay paced the floor in front of her and suddenly she was thinking about those moments before she'd seen the face in the window…those moments when she had been in his arms and had been, oh, so willing.

She now knew what it was like to be kissed thoroughly, deeply by him. She now knew what his hands felt like on her skin. And she had been so fevered by his kisses and by his touch.

If she hadn't seen the face in the window she wouldn't have stopped Clay. She would have allowed him—no, she would have encouraged him to keep kissing her, to keep touching her and to make love with her.

And that would have been a huge mistake. If his kisses were anything to go by, then making love with him would be magical and unforgettable. Then she'd want to do it again and again. He would eventually break her heart.

She supposed she should thank Robby for interrupting what had been happening. Still, not only was she disturbed by Robby's presence outside, she was also embarrassed that a student had seen her making out on her sofa like a horny teenager.

All thoughts of Clay and lovemaking flew out of her head when Dillon stepped back in the front door.

"Where's Robby?" Clay asked.

"I let him go with a stern lecture," Dillon replied. "I've really got nothing to charge him with except trespassing."

"Maybe if you threw him in jail then the threats to Miranda would stop." Clay sat down in the chair, obviously frustrated.

"I can't keep him indefinitely in a jail cell on a maybe."

"So, what was he doing here? Besides peeking in the window?" Clay asked.

"I think what we have here is a kid with a crush," Dillon replied.

"A crush?" Miranda looked at Dillon in shocked surprise.

Dillon nodded. "It took a while to get it out of him, but he finally confessed that he was worried about you after the accident and wanted to check up on you. He also told me that he thought you were the prettiest woman in the entire town."

"While I agree with his sentiments, I'm not sure I believe that's all that's going on with that kid," Clay replied. "Did you ask him if anyone else was with him?"

"I did, and he told me he was alone. He didn't want any of his friends to know that he was checking up on Miranda." Dillon sighed. "Look, I don't want to ruin a kid's life if all he's guilty of is having a crush on a pretty teacher and peeping in her window. On the other hand, I intend to put one of my deputies on him to watch what he does and where he goes for the next couple of days."

"Thanks for coming out, Dillon," she said. "It was frightening to see somebody peeking in the window." A shiver threatened to work up her spine as she thought of that moment when she'd seen the face.

"I don't think you have to worry about Robby showing up here again. I definitely put the fear of God into him." Dillon looked at Clay. "Just to be on the safe side, do you want to do a quick check around the house to make sure nothing is amiss?"

"Let's do it," Clay replied. He looked at her. "I'll lock the door behind us and knock when we're finished."

She had a sudden desire to get off the sofa and walk with them to the door. She had a desire to kiss Clay goodbye, as if she might not ever see him again. She quickly tamped it down and the men stepped outside.

She sat on the edge of the sofa to await Clay's return. Her emotions were in such a tangled mess. She wanted to blame her concussion, but she knew that wasn't the reason.

If the fact that she was a target for somebody's hatred wasn't enough, her feelings toward Clay had her brain completely muddled. Maybe it *was* still because of the brain shaking she'd gotten in the accident.

She almost dreaded Dillon leaving. When he was gone, she and Clay would be alone again and she didn't want to talk about what had happened…what had been going to happen between them. To talk about it gave it substance and she just wanted to forget it had happened.

She heard a knock and carefully got up and walked slowly to the door to allow Clay back inside. Thank goodness her ankle was now healed enough to hold her weight, although it wasn't a hundred percent back to normal.

"Thank God we didn't find anything." He relocked the door.

She walked back to the sofa. "Good, then I think I'll go ahead and get some sleep. I'm completely exhausted." She intentionally didn't meet his gaze. "And tonight I want to sleep in my own bed."

"Are you sure you're good to do the stairs?"

She finally looked at him. "My ankle is feeling much stronger, so the stairs shouldn't be a problem." With the drama over, all she felt was the need to escape from Clay.

"Okay, then I'll call it a night, too." He followed her up the stairs where she checked on Jenny and Henry. Thank goodness they were both still sound asleep and hadn't been awakened by the commotion.

She then went to her bedroom doorway and turned back to face him. "I'll see you in the morning."

He held her gaze for a long moment and she was so afraid he was going to say something about what had happened between them. She was so afraid he would try to kiss her again, and if he did, she'd be utterly lost.

"See you in the morning," he finally said and headed back up the hallway to the room where he'd been staying. She sighed in relief and went to the dresser drawer that held her night clothing. She grabbed a fresh nightgown and went into the master bathroom.

She didn't want to think about the fact that somebody obviously wanted her dead. She didn't want to speculate on whether that person was Robby.

She also didn't want to think about Clay, but

thoughts of him filled her head as she changed her clothes and got ready for bed.

His childhood had sounded horrendous. She'd been so lucky in being raised by parents who loved her, parents who had made her feel special every single day of her life.

She couldn't imagine the little boy Clay had been, a little boy who had constantly been told he was ugly and unwanted. What kind of people had raised him?

As he'd shared those things with her, her heart had cried. She'd wanted to find that little boy inside of him and pull him close to her heart. She'd wanted to tell him he was beautiful and had deserved to be loved.

Was it possible those experiences were what made him date so much? Was he somehow seeking the validation that he wasn't ugly from all the women he went out with? It was certainly possible.

She washed her face, brushed her teeth and left the bathroom and got into her own bed for the first time since the accident. The mattress seemed to welcome her like an old friend as she relaxed into it.

She desperately wanted to fall asleep, to stop thinking, but her brain continued to work overtime. She thought of Clay playing Go Fish with her children, of how he listened with interest when they talked to him and displayed infinite patience. She knew both of her children positively adored him.

Visions of them all seated at the table and laughing together also cascaded through her head, visions of happiness…of family.

Finally warmth swept through her body as she remembered his kisses and what it had felt like to be held so tightly in his arms. She stared up at the darkened ceiling and a rush of emotion swept through her as she realized what was happening.

She was precariously close to falling completely and totally in love with Romeo Clay Madison.

Chapter 9

Saturday morning Hank arrived to pick up Henry and Jenny as usual. Lori came in with him, carrying another casserole. "It's a chicken and rice dish that just needs to be warmed up."

"Lori, you didn't have to do that," Miranda protested as Clay took the food from her. "I really am feeling a lot better now."

"That's good to hear," Hank replied. "Your bruise across your forehead is almost gone."

"Thank goodness," Miranda replied. "And my ankle has healed up nicely."

"We've been worried about you," Lori said.

"I've been worrying myself sick about you,"

Hank added. "I can't believe somebody cut your brake lines."

Clay carried the casserole into the kitchen and placed it in the refrigerator, then returned to the living room where the kids and the couple were ready to leave.

"You'll let us know if Dillon finds out anything new?" Lori asked.

"I definitely want to know any news," Hank added.

"You know I'll keep you both updated," Miranda replied.

When they were all gone, Clay and Miranda returned to the kitchen where they had been having coffee. "Flint should be arriving anytime," he told her. As usual she looked good clad in a plain navy T-shirt and jeans. It didn't matter what she wore, he always found her more than beautiful.

"Flint?" She looked at him curiously.

"Flint McCay. He's one of my buddies from the ranch."

"I don't think I've ever met him," she replied.

"He's a good guy," Clay replied. "He's our star rodeo cowboy. He rides bulls and he's won a bunch of first-place medals."

"I don't think we have any bulls that need to be ridden," she said with a sparkle of humor in her eyes. "He's coming over for a visit?"

"Not really. He's actually coming over to help me build you some new porch steps and railings today."

"Oh, Clay, you don't have to do that," she protested.

"Yes, I do." He definitely needed to get out of the house and into the fresh air where he wouldn't smell her sweet fragrance. He needed to do something physical that would hopefully use up some of the adrenaline that filled him. He desperately needed to focus on something other than his simmering desire for her. That's why he had called Flint at the crack of dawn to set up the day of outside work.

"It's not that big of a job," he continued. "Somebody is eventually going to get hurt on those stairs and it might be one of the kids, and I know you don't want that."

"Of course I don't want that. Still, it's not your job to do. I intended to eventually hire somebody."

"It needs to be done and I'm here and ready." The doorbell rang and he stood. "And now Flint is here, so please, no more protests." He went to the door and opened it for the tall, lanky, blond-haired cowboy.

"Hey, Flint," Clay greeted his friend and led him into the kitchen. "This is Miranda. Miranda, this is Flint."

"Nice to meet you," Flint said and swept his black hat off his head.

"It's nice to meet you, too. I told Clay this wasn't necessary," she said.

"No offense, ma'am, but I just walked up those porch steps. I'd say a little work on them is definitely necessary," Flint replied.

"And I definitely intend to pay you both for materials and labor," she told him.

"You can figure that out with Clay," Flint responded.

"And we can talk about that later," Clay said. "Now, let's get to it." Even now, just standing close to Miranda, he wanted her. He just hoped doing this physical work would allow him to release some of the taut tension inside him. "We'll see you later," he said to Miranda, and then he and Flint left the house.

"I think I've got everything we need for the repair job." Flint eyed the stairs and railings.

Clay looked beyond Flint to the truck in the driveway that held new lumber and tools. "Thanks, man. I really appreciate the help."

"No problem," Flint replied. "And you know I don't want any money for this. I like the idea of you owing me. That way, anytime I want I can force you to muck out the stables on the days it's my job."

"We'll have to figure out how many days of mucking this job is worth," Clay said as the two men walked to the truck to unload the lumber.

"I figure at least a dozen," Flint replied.

"Ha, and I figure you're nuts." Clay laughed.

It was another bright and beautiful day and although the temperature was mild, it didn't take long for Clay to work up a sweat.

As the two worked on ripping out the old steps and railings, Flint caught him up on everything going on back at the ranch.

"Cassie hired a new guy. His name is Alex Scott and he's from Texas."

"What brings him to Bitterroot?" Clay asked curiously.

"Abe Breckinridge is his great uncle." Flint used a hammer to pound out a rotten rail spindle.

"So, why isn't he working for Abe?" Clay asked. Abe Breckinridge owned a cattle spread almost as big as the Holiday Ranch. The old man and Cass had been good friends before Cass's death.

"He said he didn't like mixing family and business," Flint replied.

"What do you think of him?"

"He seems all right. He's a good worker, but seems a bit private," Flint said and then went on to talk about other things that had happened at the ranch since Clay had been gone.

"What have you heard from Forest?" Flint asked.

Forest Stevens had been one of the boys brought to the ranch, and he had also been Clay's closest friend. When Adam Benson's murder victims' skeletons had been dug up beneath an old shed after the tornado, Dillon had called in Dr. Patience Forbes, a forensic anthropologist, to help with the case. The feisty red-head had captured Forest's heart, and when she'd gone back to Oklahoma City, Forest had gone with her.

"I talked to him last week and the big news is Patience is pregnant."

"That's great," Flint replied. "I'm sure he's over the moon about it."

They stopped talking and got busy. The two men worked well together. They had often worked together in the past to repair a variety of outbuildings on the Holiday Ranch.

It was just after noon when Miranda appeared in the front door. "Why don't you two knock off for a few minutes and come inside and eat some lunch. I just made some ham and cheese sandwiches and I've got tall glasses of iced tea."

"You sure don't have to ask me twice," Flint said and set down the hammer he'd been using.

"I'm right behind you," Clay replied.

Miranda had the table set with big sandwiches, a bag of chips and the cold drinks. They washed up at the kitchen sink and then sat to eat.

"This is really nice of you," Flint said as he grabbed a handful of chips to add to his plate.

"Goodness, it's the least I can do considering what you are doing for me. I'm just happy to get the stairs and railings fixed."

"Aren't you going to join us?" Clay asked.

"No, I'm fine. I just want to see that the two of

you are fed and watered well." She stood next to the sink and the sunshine drifting through the window danced in her hair. Geez, even eating a ham and cheese sandwich, he wanted her.

"Clay told me about everything that's happened to you," Flint said. "I hope you're doing okay."

"I'm doing much better, although I don't know what I would have done without Clay here. He's been great with my kids and has been taking good care of all of us." She smiled at him.

"It's been my pleasure," he replied and then focused on his sandwich. Since the night when they had started something that had been stopped by Robby, Clay had had trouble thinking about anything else.

They hadn't discussed it and she acted like it had never happened, which made him believe she regretted it. That night they had definitely moved out of the friend zone. And now they were back firmly in that zone. The only thing he regretted was that Robby had brought a halt to it long before Clay had wanted it to end.

He was grateful when lunch was over and the two men got back to work. He needed to keep himself busy. Surely by the end of the day he'd have better control of the longing that swept through him over and over again while he was in her presence.

"You know she's crazy about you," Flint said once they were back outside.

Clay laughed, despite the quick flutter of his heart. "I don't think so."

"I know what I saw. Man, I'm telling you, the way she looks at you when you aren't looking at her tells me she's head over heels for you."

Flint's words played and replayed through Clay's mind as the two continued to work. Was it possible she was really ready to take their relationship into something deeper?

Certainly it seemed that way on Thursday night when she'd kissed him with so much passion. Of course, he knew a man and a woman could share a wealth of physical desire that had nothing to do with love. And there was also the very real possibility that Flint was wrong. Flint's words had only managed to confuse Clay and it was a confusion that wasn't going to be resolved until Miranda made a move.

As the afternoon wore on and the heat of the day peaked, Clay took off his shirt and Flint did the same. "I didn't think it was supposed to get so hot today," Clay said.

"Yeah, and we have the possibility of some strong storms blowing through after sunset," Flint replied.

"Ah, spring," Clay replied. There was always a possibility of strong storms in Oklahoma at this time of the year and tornados seemed to love the state. Hopefully they wouldn't experience that tonight.

It was almost dinner time when the work was all finished and the men loaded Flint's truck with the old lumber and cleaned up their tools. Dark clouds had begun to gather in the southwest, promising, at the very least, a good rain shower.

Miranda stepped out and gazed at the new stairs and the sturdy railings and got teary-eyed as she looked at them.

"I don't know how to thank you both," she said.

"No need to thank me. The work got me away from the ranch for a day to work with this guy." Flint playfully wrapped an arm around Clay's neck.

Clay extricated himself from Flint's grip and grinned at Miranda. "At least now if somebody trips on the stairs you'll know it's because of their own clumsiness."

Flint said his goodbyes and minutes later Clay and Miranda were in the kitchen where she had cooked a meatloaf with mashed potatoes for dinner.

"I definitely need a shower before I sit down," he said.

"You also definitely need to tell me what I owe you for the materials and your and Flint's time," she replied.

"Okay, after I shower and eat dinner you owe me a kiss. That's the payment I demand."

Her cheeks turned a pretty shade of pink. "Clay, I'm being serious."

He grinned. "And so am I. Give me a kiss later and we'll call it even."

"Go take your shower," she said and tried to flip him with the hand towel she held.

He laughed and was still laughing as he got beneath a hot spray of water. It was so good to see the sparkle back in her eyes and to know she was feeling better. He also loved that she now felt comfortable enough to tease him.

The kids were gone for the night at Hank's and that meant he and Miranda would be completely alone. She hadn't told him no about the kiss and he definitely intended to collect from her.

By the time he got out of the shower he was starving. He wasn't hungry for meatloaf and mashed potatoes, but he did have a huge appetite for Miranda.

As she waited for Clay to get out of the shower and come back downstairs for dinner, Miranda tried to keep her mind off the night to come.

There would be a lot of alone time with Clay, and despite the fact he had been outside for most of the day he had stirred a longing inside her.

She'd spent way too much time peeking out the window and watching him work. She'd admired the bronzed beauty of his bare back and the way the muscles moved as he wielded a hammer or used a saw.

His sweat had only made his exposed muscles more prominent as it gleamed on his skin. She wanted to be in those arms again. She realized her longing for him had nothing to do with her gratitude for everything he had done for her and her children. Aside from everything else she felt about him, she wanted to have the experience of making love with him.

It shocked her. She hadn't felt as if he was consciously seducing her, but she definitely felt completely seduced. She'd sworn she wouldn't be another notch on his bedpost, but that had been before she really knew him.

He was so different from everything she had thought him to be. There was nothing vacuous about him, and the scars he bore only made him more attractive to her.

It had been so very long since she'd felt this kind of desire, this kind of longing for a man. Clay stirred feelings she'd thought she'd never feel again.

He now walked into the kitchen with damp hair and smelling of minty soap and shaving cream. "Hmm, that felt good," he said as he sat at the table. "Nothing like a nice hot shower to put things right in the world."

"I much prefer a bath," she responded. "With lots of bubbles."

She fixed him a plate and set it before him. "I hope you're hungry."

His blue eyes gazed at her with an intensity that made her breath catch in the back of her throat. "Trust me, I'm starving," he replied.

She held his gaze for a moment longer. "You have to stop looking at me that way," she said, appalled that her voice sounded all breathy.

Those eyes of his seemed to smile at her before his lips moved upward. "What way?"

Warmth filled her cheeks. "You know what way… like I'm a piece of cheesecake and you love that for dessert."

He laughed. "There is no way I'd look at you like you're a piece of cake. When I look at you all I see is a beautiful, desirable woman who is strong and brave. And now, are you going to sit down and enjoy this meal with me?"

She plated her food and joined him at the table. "The clouds are really starting to build up. Looks like it's going to be a stormy night," she said in an effort to get her mind off the wonderful words he had just spoken.

"Are you afraid of storms?" he asked.

"Not really, unless there's a tornado threat. Sometimes I like a good bout of thunder and lightning and rain."

"What about the kids?"

"Jenny is like me. Storms don't bother her at all, but Henry gets scared by the thunder." She frowned as she thought of her little boy.

"I'm sure Lori and Hank will soothe him if he gets scared," Clay said softly, as if he'd read her mind and knew her concerns.

"I'm sure you're right," she agreed. Still, the idea of her little boy being frightened and her not being there to wrap him in her arms and make him feel safe brought up the thought that somebody had tried to take her away from her children forever. And that somebody was still out there with that intention in mind.

When would the person try to come after her again? What would they do next? She'd survived two attacks relatively unscathed. Would she be so lucky when the third attempt happened?

"What about you? How do you feel about storms?" she asked in an attempt to guide her mind away from such horrifying thoughts.

He hesitated for a long moment. "I guess I'm a little bit ambivalent about them. On the one hand they really don't bother me at all, but occasionally they bring back memories of my mother leaving. It was storming on the last night that she tucked me into bed, the last time I saw her."

She reached out and touched the back of his hand. "I'm sorry, Clay."

He shrugged. "It was just something that happened to me. It didn't define who I am or what I have become."

"And you've become a wonderful man," she replied.

At the moment she couldn't imagine him not being here with her. His presence allowed her to

sleep well at night knowing that he was here to protect her.

Other than Robby peeking in through her window, things had been quiet. But she couldn't forget
that she was still at risk. She looked out the window, her thoughts churning like the dark clouds of
the approaching storm.

Except for going to the ball game for Henry, she'd
been housebound. But she couldn't stay inside forever. And Clay couldn't stay here forever.

"Hey." His voice pulled her to look back at him.
"I don't like the thoughts that are going around in
your head right now."

"How do you know what thoughts I'm having?"

"When you are having troubling thoughts a little
telling frown appears right between your eyebrows."

She sighed and set down her fork. "I was just
thinking about the attacks and you."

"Me?" He looked at her in surprise. "What about
me?"

"You can't stay here forever, Clay. You have a
life to get back to. And I can't stay in hiding in this
house forever. It's not fair to my children who have
all kinds of summer activities planned once school
is out."

"Let's just take things one day at a time for now,"
he replied. He hesitated a moment and his eyes darkened slightly. "I don't think it's going to take forever for the person who wants to harm you to act

again. I think another attack is going to happen fairly quickly."

"Are you trying to make me feel better?" she asked dryly.

"No, I'm trying to be honest with you. You were attacked on a Friday night and then again on the following Monday. I think whoever it is is impatient, and that means the person will attack sooner rather than later. And now I think we should find a more pleasant topic."

"I'm feeling much better, and that means I get to be the boss, and I'm not finished talking about it all yet," she replied.

He grinned at her. "What crazy fool told you that you get to be boss when you are feeling better?"

"You're the crazy fool, and don't tease with me when I'm trying to be serious."

"Okay." His smile fell away. "I'm sorry. I always want you to speak what's on your mind."

"Trust me, I usually do." She picked up her fork once again and drew the tines through the mashed potatoes on her plate as her thoughts took her back to dark places. "But what if the person after me does have patience? What if they have plenty of patience? What if nothing happens and then your vacation is over?"

"Then I'll go to work during the day and come back here each night. I'm fairly comfortable that nobody can get through your locks. As long as you don't open the door to anyone while I'm gone then you should be fine."

"And if I need to go out during the day? Jenny and Henry don't deserve to be housebound during the summer days."

He set his fork down and released a deep sigh. "Then we'll figure something out. I still have a full week of vacation left and if I need more time off work I'm sure it wouldn't be a problem."

"I'm sure you have things you'd rather be doing than staying here."

"Actually, that's not true. What could be better than spending my time with a beautiful woman? As a bonus, I get to hang out with her incredible kids. I can't think of anything else I'd rather be doing."

He looked so earnest that some of her fears faded away. He was right. She had to take things one day at a time right now, otherwise she'd make herself completely crazy.

They finished eating dinner, cleaned up the kitchen and moved into the living room where a new tension built up between them.

They sat on the sofa and made small talk, but all she could think about was that they were alone in the house, without the children. According to what he had said earlier, she owed him a kiss. She knew if he got that kiss it was very possible things would spiral out of control, and there was a part of her that wanted it, that yearned to lose control with him.

At eight o'clock they turned on a crime drama show and the first signs of the storm sounded overhead. Distant thunder could be heard above the volume of the television.

"Sounds like we're going to get some rain," she said.

"We can use it. So far it's been a fairly dry spring." He moved closer to her on the sofa. "You know when this show is over I'm going to demand my payment for my work today." He spoke the words slowly, his voice slightly deeper than usual.

A delicious warmth swept through her body. She stared at the television, but couldn't have said what happened next in the show they were watching. All she could think about was being in his arms again and kissing his delicious lips.

By the time the crime drama was done the storm was upon them. Thunder boomed overhead and lightning lit the night skies.

"Want to watch another show?" she asked.

"No." He stood and stretched with his arms overhead and then dropped them and held out a hand to her. His gaze slid to her lips and paused there, and a slow smile curved his mouth. "I'm in the mood to get paid. Are you ready to pay me for all my hard labor today?"

She hesitated, unsure that her legs would hold her considering she was suddenly breathless. Then she nodded, took his hand and allowed him to pull her up off the sofa and close to his chest.

Leaning into him, she gave him a quick peck on the cheek. "There, you're paid," she said.

He laughed, his eyes sparkling brightly. "That doesn't even pay me for my first hour on the job."

She knew what he wanted and she wanted to give it to him. She wanted to give him a kiss that would weaken *his* knees and make him as breathless as she already felt.

Raising her arms to wrap around his neck, she touched his lower lip with her tongue and then covered his mouth with hers. He released a startled gasp and tightened his arms around her waist.

She was the one who deepened the kiss by swirling her tongue with his. He moaned, the sound a guttural growl in the back of his throat that sent her senses reeling.

He finally tore his mouth from hers and trailed kisses down the length of her neck. "Miranda." Her name was a fevered whisper near her ear. "I want you. I want you so badly."

This was the moment for her to stop things if they were going to be stopped. She knew there was a possibility he was going to break her heart. She also knew that making love with him would probably mean way more to her than it would to him.

But there was no part of her heart or mind that wanted to call a halt. She raised her head and looked into his beautiful blue eyes. "I want you, too," she whispered.

His eyes deepened in hue and he covered her mouth with his in a searing kiss as a roll of thunder sounded overhead. When he ended the kiss he scooped her into his arms and carried her up the stairs to the bedroom where he'd been staying.

He set her down next to the bed in the darkened room, and when lightning momentarily lit it she saw the raw hunger on his features.

Delight shivered up her spine. She had never felt this way about a man before, as if he was the food she needed to eat, the very air she needed to breathe.

She pulled her T-shirt over her head and dropped it on the floor. She was eager to be naked and in his arms, and to that end she quickly continued to undress as he did the same.

Within minutes they were both naked and in the bed, their legs tangled together as they kissed. Her skin loved the feel of his as her hands stroked up and down his broad back. Muscles played beneath his skin and she delighted at the feel of them.

His hands were everywhere…caressing her back and then tangling in her hair. Each touch stole her breath away as all her nerve endings came alive after being dormant for years. She'd never, ever felt this way before; she'd never felt so utterly alive before.

"You are so beautiful," he whispered after a bright lightning flash.

His hands moved to cover her breasts and she gasped in pleasure as his fingers captured her nipples. He followed with his mouth, his tongue dancing and playing with first one turgid peak and then the other. The lightning outside had nothing to do with the electricity that sizzled through her.

He kissed her again, the kiss dizzying her senses. It was impossible to think of anything but him. His hands were hot against her skin as he caressed her back...her breasts...and her hips.

When his hand moved down her body to touch her as intimately as a man could touch a woman, she once again gasped in delight. He knew just how to stroke her, what pressure to use and how to move to bring her the most exquisite pleasure.

The flames inside her burned hotter and hotter until she thought she might spontaneously combust. Then came the magnificent waves of her orgasm, which left her weak and crying out his name over and over again.

He scarcely gave her time to recover. He grabbed a condom from where he'd placed it on the nightstand and rolled it on, then poised himself between her thighs. His pretty-boy features looked savage, wild in the flash of lightning that lit the room. Thunder boomed and rain pelted the windows, but all she cared about was Clay.

"I can't wait, Miranda. I need you right now."

To answer him she arched upward and grabbed

hold of his taut buttocks. He eased into her and she shuddered with a new pleasure.

He began to move against her, into her with slow, smooth strokes. But as he increased the speed her passion once again rose. Faster and faster he moved and higher and higher she climbed until she reached a peak and then fell over it, gasping and sobbing as sweet sensations swept through her.

He immediately stiffened against her and cried out her name as he reached his climax, as well. He held himself above her on his elbows and took her lips in a gentle kiss that misted her eyes with tears. Then his gaze warmed her as he stared down at her. "That was beyond amazing," he whispered.

"I agree," she replied, still breathless from what she'd just experienced.

She had never felt so loved as she did in this moment. It was as if she had waited all her life for Clay. He kissed her one more time and then rolled off her and onto his feet. "I'll be right back," he said and went into the bathroom across the hall.

She stared at the ceiling overhead as a distant rumble of thunder sounded. The storm was moving away, although a soft rain continued to fall and pattered against the window. She felt like dancing in the rain, a joyous dance of complete fulfillment.

Clay came back into the bedroom and crawled back into the bed with her. "It's still raining," he said as he pulled her back into his warm embrace.

"I know... I was just thinking that I'd like to go outside and dance in it."

"We should go over to Halena's house. Rumor has it she dances naked in the rain," he replied with a chuckle.

Miranda laughed as she thought about the colorful Choctaw woman. "I wonder if she wears a hat?"

"I'm sure she does. She probably has special little rain hats just for the occasion." He leaned up on one elbow at her side and trailed a finger down the side of her face. "And speaking about special...this... us...is special."

His words spilled a happiness, a joy through her and she knew in that moment that she was completely in love with Clay Madison.

Was it possible she really was the Juliet to his Romeo?

She wanted to see him up close. She desperately wanted to talk to him. But she knew what was going on with Miranda Silver. She knew the woman was in trouble. She just hadn't thought about him moving in with her.

She should have made her move earlier. With Clay cooped up in Miranda's house all day and all night, talking to him had been impossible. She had been parked down the street day and night, just waiting for an opportunity...waiting for the right moment to act.

Now, sitting in the rain down the block from Miranda's home, she tried to figure out what her next move would be. She had a feeling she'd only have one shot at getting what she wanted. It was imperative that she got it right.

Chapter 10

They made love again just after dawn. It was a slow, languid loving-making that left Clay more satisfied than he'd ever felt in his life.

Afterward, when she left his bed to start her morning, Clay remained stretched out on the sheets that now smelled of her sweet fragrance. It made him reluctant to rise and face the day.

Making love with her had been some kind of wonderful. He'd felt more intimately, more emotionally connected to her than he had to any other woman he'd ever been with.

She is the one.

The words thundered in his head.

And scared the holy hell out of him.

She is your Juliet.

The voice in his head thundered once again.

He frowned, suddenly confused by his own feelings. Wasn't this what he wanted? A woman who would intrigue him with her thoughts every day of his life? A woman who would stir a passion inside him, not only to make love with her, but also to share his laughter and his dreams?

That's how he felt about Miranda, so why did the idea of making a future with her scare him so badly? Why was he reluctant to even acknowledge the depth of his feelings for her? It didn't make any sense.

The scent of freshly brewed coffee and frying bacon finally roused him to sit on the edge of the bed. It was time to get dressed and go downstairs.

Time.

He felt like maybe he just needed a little time to process everything going on inside his own heart. His feelings about her had jumped into his brain so suddenly.

He chided himself. Hell, it was just in the last couple of days that she'd been able to smile at him without a touch of wariness in her eyes. She couldn't be the one if she didn't want to be the one. Just because she'd gone to bed with him didn't mean she was in love with him.

He took a quick shower, got dressed and headed down to the kitchen where she stood in front of the stove. Clad in a short pink terry robe and with her hair pulled up in a messy ponytail she looked utterly charming.

He must have made a noise because she whirled around, and when she saw him a beautiful smile curved her lips. "Good morning."

"Back at you," he replied and walked over to the counter where the coffeepot was located.

"I hope you're hungry. I've got biscuits finishing up in the oven and gravy ready to go with the bacon and eggs."

"Wow, sounds like a feast. Anything I can do to help?" He poured himself a cup of coffee.

"Just stay out of my way. You've cooked so many breakfasts for us, now it's my turn to cook for you." She turned back to the stove and began to remove the bacon from the skillet.

"I'm glad to see you feeling so much better." He sat at the table.

"I feel so good I feel guilty about not going in to work tomorrow. It's the last day of school, and even though I'm not teaching, I'd really like to show up there for a couple of hours just to say goodbye to everyone for the summer."

He frowned thoughtfully. "I guess we could arrange that. I could drop you off, and while you're at the school I could head back to the ranch and check up on things there."

Actually he wouldn't mind a little time away from

her to sort out his thoughts and feelings where she was concerned. He had to figure out why, if he really thought she was the one, the idea scared him so badly. Was it because he feared that she wouldn't feel the same way about him?

Thankfully, she wasn't a woman who needed to chew over what they had shared the night before and again that morning. As they ate breakfast she talked about the summer plans she had for Jenny and Henry.

"They always do two weeks of the day program at the Community Center in July. They really enjoy that," she said. "They do all kinds of crafts there."

"Jerod always works at the center for those two weeks," Clay replied, referencing one of the other cowboys from the Holiday Ranch.

She smiled. "The kids all adore Jerod even though he can be stern with them."

"Yeah, he's definitely one of the good guys. I like to believe that all of us lost boys grew up to be good guys," he replied.

By the time they finished breakfast and she had showered and dressed for the day, Clay once again felt the need to distance himself from her.

Minutes later he was outside and pushing her lawnmower to cut the grass, a task made slightly difficult due to the rain the night before. He kept himself busy outside with yard work for most of the morning.

He went in at noon to eat lunch and then was back outside using clippers to cut back the bushes around the house. As much as he loved being with Miranda and the children, he'd missed being outside.

Since the moment he had arrived on Cass's ranch, he'd enjoyed being on the back of a horse with the sunshine on his shoulders. If he got to the ranch tomorrow for a couple of hours, the first thing he intended to do was get on his horse, Rowdy, and ride the range.

He was a cowboy who had never really wanted to do or be anything else after Cass had mentored him and he grew older. And he was perfectly satisfied working for Cassie on the Holiday spread. If he and Miranda did make a go of things, he would still want to work the ranch during the days and then come home to this house with Miranda and the children to spend the nights.

As he worked on the lawn he kept his gaze shooting around the area, wanting to make sure that nobody got close to the house or somehow sneaked up on him.

Miranda's attacker was never far from his mind. He felt the tick of a clock deep in his chest, a clock counting down to another assault.

An acid attack…then car sabotage…what might come next? A bomb thrown through the window? A sniper on the roof of a nearby home? Dammit, who in the hell was behind the attacks?

He set down the clippers he'd been using and looked up and down the street. There was only one car parked against the curb down the block. He didn't know who the black sedan belonged to, but he'd seen it parked there almost every day that he'd been here. It had Texas plates so he assumed somebody was visiting from out of town.

A familiar truck appeared, coming down the street. As it pulled up to the curb Clay grinned and walked to the passenger window.

"Hey, Tony. What's up?" Tony Nakni was Mary's husband and one of Clay's "brothers" from the ranch.

"I'm in town getting supplies and thought I'd swing by here. We miss seeing your ugly mug at the ranch."

Clay laughed. "You only wish you had an ugly mug like mine," he replied.

"So, how are things going here?"

"Good. At least, nothing bad has happened since the car accident, although I'm always on the lookout for trouble."

Tony frowned. "Dillon still hasn't figured anything out?"

"There's nothing to help him figure it out. No clues, no real suspects, it's frustrating as hell."

"All the cowboys at the ranch have been trying to figure out who might have a problem with Miranda, but none of us have been able to name a single person. Thinking about all the women you've dated in the past gave us all headaches and so we just gave up."

"Ha-ha."

Tony grinned. "So, how are things going between you and Miranda?"

It was Clay's turn to frown. "Confusing." He hesitated a moment and then continued, "I think she's the one, Tony, but I'm also thinking maybe I'm not really ready for it like I thought I was."

Tony looked at him in surprise. "I thought you wanted to find the woman who would be *the* woman in your life. For the last year that's what you've been talking about. Why don't you think you're ready for it?"

Clay hesitated again before replying. He wasn't about to admit to Tony that he was scared and didn't really know what he was scared about. "I don't know what's going on with me," he finally said.

"What about Miranda? How does she feel about you?"

Clay thought about the passion she had shared with him the night before and her warm smiles this morning. "I think she's falling for me."

"Then you should be happy," Tony replied.

"I know, and there's a part of me that is, but there's another part of me that just wants to escape." He frowned again, feeling as if he was baring his soul. "Don't worry. I'll figure it out."

"Clay, I know it's tough to put your heart on the

line, but take it from me, the risk is worth it. I was scared to death to risk giving my heart to Mary, but I'm so glad I did because I can't imagine my life without her now. If you think Miranda is falling for you, then you'd better figure it out fast."

"I know," Clay replied. "It's just…it's all happened so fast."

Tony laughed. "That's the way it happens. All of a sudden you realize you're crazy in love."

Clay grinned at his friend. "Right now I just feel crazy."

The men visited for a few more minutes and then Tony left and Clay went back to clipping bushes that really didn't need his attention.

What in the hell was wrong with him? He cared about Miranda more than he'd ever cared about another woman, so what was holding him back?

At five o'clock he went inside for dinner. The house smelled of lemon polish, cleaners and garlic and tomatoes. She'd obviously been as busy inside the house all day as he had been outside.

"Something smells delicious," he said as he entered the kitchen.

"Homemade spaghetti meat sauce," she said. She gestured to the table. "It's all ready to serve."

"Good, because I'm hungry." He went to the sink and washed his hands. "Is there anything I can do?"

"If you want to grab the salad from the fridge, I'll get the spaghetti and the garlic bread on the plates."

Moments later they were seated at the table. "You spent a lot of time outside today," she said.

"The lawn needed a lot of work," he replied without making eye contact with her. "It's a good thing I found all the tools I needed in your garage."

"Hank didn't take any of the lawn equipment with him when he left. I think Lori pays somebody to mow the yard where they live now." She hesitated and looked down at her plate. She then looked back at him and continued, "If I didn't know better I'd think that you were avoiding me all day."

He felt the weight of her gaze on him and he looked up at her and smiled. It was impossible for him not to smile at her. Clad in a yellow T-shirt and white jeans, she looked like a ray of sunshine seated across from him. He couldn't help the way his heart warmed at the sight of her.

"I wasn't avoiding you. The lawn needed to be taken care of," he replied. It was a half lie. He had been avoiding her, but the grass had really needed to be mowed.

Just sitting across from her he wanted her again. He not only wanted to make love with her, but he couldn't imagine not sitting across from her at the breakfast and dinner table every day of his life. He was in love with her.

She was his Juliet. So why was he so damned confused?

* * *

Dinner was…awkward. Clay was quiet and any conversation they shared seemed a bit forced. It had never been this way between them before and it made her nervous.

He didn't know about her feelings but her heart was now forever his. And she believed she'd seen love in his eyes so often in the last couple of days and also thought she'd felt it radiating from him when they'd made love the night before and again that morning.

She definitely wasn't feeling the love at the moment. She wanted to ask him what was going on, but before she got a chance Hank arrived with the children in tow.

"The yard looks good," Hank said begrudgingly as the kids ran inside the house to greet Clay. "In fact, it looks better than I ever remember it looking."

"Clay worked on it all day."

Hank looked at her for several long moments. "You've got feelings for him, don't you?"

She thought about lying, but quickly decided to be honest. After all, she wasn't ashamed of how she felt for Clay. "I do," she replied.

"I hope he isn't going to break your heart," Hank replied and then smiled at her sadly. "I gave you enough heartache throughout our marriage. You didn't deserve it then and you don't deserve any more heartache for the rest of your life."

"Thanks, Hank, for saying that." It was the first time he'd really acknowledged how he had hurt her.

"You know all I want is for you to be happy, Miranda, and if he makes you happy then I hope he's crazy, madly in love with you."

She smiled at her ex-husband. "Me, too."

"At least he's good with the kids and they like him. They talk about him a lot when we have them."

"And the kids like Lori, too. I'd say in that aspect we've been lucky," she replied.

"Speaking of…she's waiting for me in her car. I'll talk to you later in the week."

Lori was parked at the curb in her old dark-blue Ford Fiesta. Miranda waved to her, and she and Hank said their goodbyes.

She locked the door and then went into the kitchen where Clay had set up a game for them all to play.

Once again, as she watched the easy and loving way Clay interacted with her children, she knew that he'd won her heart completely.

Still, even playing the game he appeared a bit distant with her. Was this what he did after he made love with a woman? Did he immediately start to cool off and begin to look for an escape from any emotional entanglement? Or was she simply misreading him and being too sensitive?

He'd worked hard outside all day. Maybe he was just tired. She got crabby when she was tired. Maybe he got quiet and withdrawn when he was tired. She told herself she shouldn't read anything into his current mood.

"I'd like to go to the school around ten tomorrow if that works for you," she said after tucking the kids into bed for the night. "Then you could pick me up around twelve-thirty?"

"Sounds good to me," he said agreeably. "And on that note I think I'm going to call it a day. All that yard work made me more tired than usual."

"Hank said the yard looks better than it ever has," she replied. "Thank you for all your hard work. I really appreciate it."

"No problem." He reached out for her and drew her into his arms. "I definitely need a good-night kiss."

She smiled. "And I'm more than happy to give you one."

His kiss was soft and gentle and soothed some of the fears she'd entertained all day. When the kiss ended he smiled down at her and gently swiped a strand of hair from her forehead.

"Sleep well and I'll see you in the morning," he said, and then he headed upstairs.

Ten minutes later she went up the stairs. His room was dark as she went past it. What she'd have liked to do was climb into his bed and sleep with his arms around her.

But she walked past his doorway and went into her own bedroom. He'd given her mixed messages, first by seemingly avoiding her all day and then by sharing a kiss with her that had tasted of love.

She changed into her nightclothes and got into bed, her mind whirling with thoughts of Clay. She was shocked to realize the depth of her love for him. She couldn't remember feeling this way about Hank, and she had given him two children.

She felt as if Clay had been seducing her since the first night when he'd bought her and her children cupcakes. He'd continued the seduction each and every day he'd been here. Now that she was thoroughly seduced, would he move on from her?

Was he really a love-them-and-leave-them kind of man? That's what she'd believed before she had gotten to know him. If that really was who he was, then he had fooled her completely.

Her heart squeezed tight at the thought of not having him in their lives anymore. If he didn't have any real feelings for her, then having him remain here for her protection would not only be awkward but would also keep her heartbreak fresh and raw every single day until something broke in the case and an arrest occurred. She didn't even want to think about how upset the kids would be if he walked out of their lives.

She finally fell asleep and into a mixture of dreams. One minute she was safe in Clay's arms and then that vision would melt away and she was running down the street with a dark figure chasing her. The figure carried either a canister of what she knew was acid or a big knife that gleamed wickedly in the moonlight.

Twice she woke up gasping in fear only to finally fall back asleep again and into the same horrific nightmares. Thankfully her final dream of the night was one of safety in Clay's big, strong arms.

She awakened the next morning later than usual. She grabbed her robe, pulled it around her, and hurried down the stairs where Clay was in the process of sending the kids out the door to the bus stop.

"Oh, wow, I overslept," she said once the kids were gone.

He smiled at her. "You must have needed the extra rest."

"I guess, but now I'd better scoot upstairs and shower and get dressed for heading over to the school."

"Do you want some breakfast? I can cook something for you while you get ready."

She smiled at him. "You are as handy as a pocket in a shirt, Mr. Clay. Thanks, but I don't need any breakfast."

"And you, Ms. Silver, are as beautiful as a rainbow in the sky. Now, go do what you need to do so I can get you to the school by ten."

Her heart was lighter than it had been the night before as she went back up the stairs. His gaze had been filled with a warmth that had covered her like a welcome blanket on a cold night. He might not be in love with her yet, but when he looked at her that way she believed eventually they would have a future together.

It was nine-thirty when she came back down the stairs wearing a pair of her black dress slacks and a crisp white blouse with oversized black buttons. Her makeup was subtle and her hair was neat and tidy. It was as if this was just another day at school, but today she would say her goodbyes to students and fellow teachers. And today she had a bodyguard dropping her off and picking her up.

Clay sat at the kitchen table and stood when she entered. "Wow, you look nice."

She warmed as his gaze swept her from head to feet. "Thanks. I guess I'm all ready to go."

Minutes later they were in his truck and headed to the high school. It was another beautiful day with the sun shining in a bright blue, cloudless sky.

"It feels good to be out of the house," she said. "I'm sure you'll enjoy being out at the ranch."

"I have to admit I'm looking forward to giving my horse a good run."

"I'm sure your horse probably misses you."

"And I'm sure Rowdy has been fine without me."

"Clay, I really appreciate what you're doing for me."

He flashed her a quick, dimpled smile. "I know that and it's been more than my pleasure."

Her love for him buoyed up inside of her, rich and deep. Her heart was filled with it, making it impossible to think of anything else.

He pulled up in front of the school and parked at the curb. "I'll be back for you around twelve-thirty. Make sure you wait until you see my truck before you leave the school building. Wait for me and I'll come inside to walk you out."

"I'll wait for you." She got out of the truck and closed the door. "Clay?" She leaned into the open passenger window. "I just want you to know that I'm madly in love with you."

He gave her a look of stunned horror. She didn't wait for him to say anything. His expression said it all. She whirled around and hurried toward the school's front door. When she reached it, he pulled away from the curb.

She remained in the doorway and watched him go, the vision of his expression haunting her. Damn. Damn. She should have never said it out loud. But her love for him had been too big to hold in.

She'd been stupid to tell him. His face hadn't read anything close to joy when she'd told him how she felt. Her heart fell to the ground, but she needed to keep it together in order to get through the next couple of hours.

Maybe she'd mistaken his physical desire for her for love. Perhaps she'd mistaken his protection of her for more than the actions of a friend.

God, she couldn't get his look of horror out of her head. Some of the joy that had filled her heart only moments before seeped away.

She was just about to turn around and head down the hallway when her eyes were captured by a familiar car pulling up to the curb outside.

Lori? What was she doing here?

The dark-haired woman opened her car door and waved wildly to Miranda. Miranda stepped outside. "The school just called Hank. Henry fell and hit his head at school and you need to get to the hospital right away."

Henry? Hurt?

Miranda's heart clenched tightly and she didn't hesitate. She ran toward Lori's car. She jumped into the passenger seat and Lori roared away from the curb.

"Where's Hank?" Miranda asked.

"Unfortunately he's in no condition to handle this," Lori replied. "You should know how that goes."

"Did they say how badly Henry was hurt?" Miranda's heart pounded a million beats a minute. All she wanted at the moment was her little boy in her arms.

"No, just that he had fallen and had been taken to the hospital," Lori replied.

It had obviously been more than a scrape or a

bruise for him to have been taken to the hospital. Oh, God, how badly had he been hurt?

"Why didn't they call me?" Miranda asked as her brain tried to make sense of things.

"They said they tried. Maybe they called your landline. I rushed over to your house but before I got there I saw Clay's truck pulling away and I followed him." She gave Miranda a quick glance. "I wish I could tell you more but that's all the information they told me."

"Oh, God, I hope he isn't hurt badly." Tears of worry burned at her eyes.

"That makes two of us," Lori replied. She pointed to her purse on the passenger side floor. "Would you mind getting my purse and handing me the syringe inside? I didn't have time to give myself my shot before I ran out of the house."

Miranda looked at her in surprise. "Are you diabetic?"

Lori nodded. "Have been for the past three years. It runs in my family."

"Are you sure you want me rummaging around in your purse?" Miranda asked. Most women were quite proprietary about their purses.

"Really, I don't mind. The syringe should be right on top. I threw it in as I left the house."

She was right. It was the first thing Miranda saw. She pulled it out and handed it to Lori. "Thanks,"

Lori said and placed it in her lap. "I'll use it as soon as I stop the car at the hospital."

Miranda nodded absently. She was consumed by thoughts of her son. Nothing else mattered more than getting to him as soon as possible. He was probably crying and wanted his mommy. Unless he was unconscious. The thought made her heart skip a few beats.

She nearly cried out in relief as the hospital came into view. *Hang on, Henry. Mommy is almost there.* She shot up a million prayers, hoping the school had overreacted to the real severity of the injury. Maybe sending him to the hospital had been nothing more than a precautionary measure and Henry was really okay. Oh, she wanted that. She wanted…no, she needed him to be okay.

As they approached the entrance to the hospital Lori stepped on the gas and flew right by it.

"Lori! What are you doing?" Miranda asked in alarm. "Why didn't you turn into the hospital?" She reached out to grab the steering wheel, but Lori slapped her hands away.

"Stop it," Lori exclaimed. "You'll make us wreck."

"What are you doing?" Miranda repeated, scream-ing the question in fear.

Lori reached over and jammed the needle into Miranda's arm. "Wha…what is going on?" Miranda grabbed the now-empty syringe from her arm. She turned to find the door handle only to discover there was none on the inside. It had been removed.

She needed to get out! Lori had obviously lost her mind. She needed to somehow stop Lori's car, but whatever was in the syringe, Miranda immediately began to feel the effect.

A deep heaviness took over her body. Lori. Oh, God, she'd never thought about Lori. None of them had thought about Lori. Why was the woman doing this? Miranda had never done anything to her.

As Miranda's mind began to fuzz over, the one thought that screamed through the cotton wrapping around her brain was that she was in trouble. She was in terrible trouble.

Chapter 11

I just want you to know that I'm in madly in love with you.

Her words had stunned him. As Clay pulled into the ranch, her shocking admission still played over and over again in his mind.

He hadn't seen that coming from her. Oh, he'd known she cared deeply about him, but he'd had no idea that she was already in love with him. She'd made it even more real by telling him how she felt.

And now he had to figure out what he was going to do about it. He knew she wasn't a woman who gave away her heart lightly and he knew what a gift she had given to him.

Was he going to take good care of her heart or was he going to break it? As he saddled up his horse, he was almost grateful that none of the other men were around.

He didn't want to talk. He wasn't feeling sociable. He needed to think and there was no better time to think than while riding Rowdy alone across the ranch.

He rode to a pasture they rarely used, hoping to assure himself some solitary time. Rowdy was unusually frisky, as if responding to Clay's unsettled thoughts.

He raced hell bent for leather toward a distant stand of trees, the morning breeze cooling his face and nearly blowing off his hat. He reached up and set it more firmly on his head and then continued to ride fast.

When he reached the trees he pulled back on the reins and Rowdy instantly obeyed the command to slow down. He walked the horse for a few minutes to cool him down and then dismounted. He threw himself into the lush grass beneath one of the trees and then stared up at the canopy of leaves overhead.

Since that first rather awkward evening when he'd bought her and Jenny and Henry cupcakes she had enchanted him. Each and every moment he spent with her had only made his feelings grow deeper.

He believed he could talk to her every single day of his life and never grow tired of listening to her.

He loved the way her mind worked and the sound of her laughter. She pulled out of him a softness he never knew he possessed. And he loved the fact that she was a wonderful mother.

Suddenly thoughts of Miranda faded away and instead his head filled with a vision of his own mother the last time he'd seen her. She'd been wearing a pair of jeans and a pink T-shirt. Her white-blond hair had been curly and appeared like a halo in the light that had spilled into his bedroom from the hallway light.

He'd thought Violet Madison was the most beautiful woman in the universe. Her blue eyes had warmed him with love and she'd smelled like her namesake.

His heart squeezed tight as memories continued to cascade through his head. He remembered the two of them stretched out in a field of clover, looking for figures in the fluffy white clouds that danced overhead. She'd been his first dance partner as they danced in their barn to the music from an old radio.

She'd taught him his alphabet before he started school. She'd explained about worms and ants and bugs they might find while they dug for hidden treasure in the garden. And there was always treasure because she'd plant either a small toy or a bagful of candy for him to find.

She had been his first real love and she'd left him. It was far too easy to tap into the emotions he'd felt that horrible morning when his father had told him she was gone and that he'd been too ugly for her to want to take him with her.

Eight-year-old Clay had been physically sick as pain had rocked through him. Gone? How could she be gone? What had filled him had been the pain of an emptiness so huge it threatened to swallow him. It had been a grief so enormous it had gutted him.

For a week he'd gone to bed every night with the hope that when he got up the next morning she'd magically be there again. He'd desperately wanted to wake up and discover that her leaving him had just been a terrible nightmare.

But as the days passed and she didn't return, the hollow winds of utter abandonment had blown through him. Abandonment. He'd vowed long ago that he would never be abandoned again, that he'd never love a woman that deeply again.

He frowned and sat up. Was that what was keeping him from fully accepting the love he knew he felt for Miranda? As deeply as he loved her, was he afraid that she would somehow abandon him like his mother had?

The little-boy dread collided with the adult man's love for Miranda. Love trumped childish fears. He wanted Miranda in his life forever and he would never have an opportunity to have that if he didn't take a leap of faith. And he so wanted to take that leap of faith with her.

He jumped up from the ground and remounted

Rowdy. He galloped back to the stable as his heart beat a rhythm of pure joy.

He loved Miranda Silver and he wanted to tell her that as soon as possible. He couldn't wait until he was supposed to pick her up from the school after noon. He needed to go there now and tell her that he loved her and wanted to build a future with her.

When he reached the stable Mac was there. "Hey, Clay. I didn't know you were here today."

"I'm here, but I'm leaving." Clay dismounted. "Can you do me a favor? Can you give Rowdy a brush down and stable him? I'm kind of in a hurry."

"Sure, no problem." Mac took Rowdy's reins from Clay. "What's the emergency?"

"I need to tell a woman that I'm in love with her," Clay said over his shoulder as he headed out of the stable.

"Go get her, cowboy," Mac yelled after him with a laugh.

Clay intended to. He fully intended to claim his woman. He raced for his truck and within minutes he was back on the road and headed back to the school. His heart sang like the tires on the truck against the blacktop.

Without his little boy fear, his heart was fully open to love without reservation. He couldn't go back in time and magically fix the abandonment he had felt when his mother had left him. But he was no longer a little boy.

He was a grown man who knew what he wanted. He wanted to build a future with Miranda and her children. He wanted to be the man in her life, the person she could depend on, the person who would always be there for her, no matter what she needed or wanted. If he was Romeo, then she was definitely his Juliet.

He'd said nothing earlier when she'd surprised him by telling him she was in love with him. He'd been so shocked words had momentarily failed him. And now that he thought about it, there had been pain on her face when she'd turned to go into the school.

She probably believed he didn't love her. Maybe she now was thinking that she was just another woman he'd dated but he was ready to move on and date somebody else. Maybe she now believed that he was really nothing more than his reputation.

He had to tell her he loved her and he had to tell her *now*. He couldn't wait another minute. He pulled up in front of the school and parked at the curb. He didn't intend to be here long…just long enough to tell Miranda Silver he was madly in love with her and wanted her to be in his life forever.

His heart still beat a tattoo of joy as he entered the glass-enclosed office. The school secretary, Abbie Lauper, smiled at him. Abbie was an older woman, a widow Clay had helped on a couple of occasions, loading groceries into her truck.

"Clay Madison, haven't ever seen your face in this building before," she said.

"I'm here looking for Miranda. I dropped her off earlier. She wanted to come in and tell some of her students and fellow teachers goodbye for the summer."

Abbie frowned and pushed her wire-rimmed glasses more fully onto the bridge of her nose. "I haven't seen her this morning, but maybe she didn't stop to sign in as a visitor and instead went right to her classroom. That's not like Miranda. She always abides by the rules and knows she should check in here since she isn't officially teaching her class today."

"Where is her room?" Clay asked.

"Second floor, room 210. Stairs are straight ahead as you leave the office and turn left."

"Thanks, Abbie." He hurried out of the office and headed for the stairs. He took them two at a time and then walked down the hallway to room 210.

A young woman he didn't know stood at the front of the classroom. She was obviously the substitute teacher who had been hired to fill in for Miranda. There was no sign of the woman he most definitely wanted to see.

"Has anyone seen Ms. Silver this morning?" he asked.

A chorus of voices, including the teacher's, said

"No." For the first time Clay's heart began to beat a different rhythm…one of controlled alarm.

He tried to keep his disquiet tamped down. Didn't most schools have a lounge for the teachers? Maybe she was there, visiting with teachers as they came in and out.

"Can anyone tell me where the teachers' lounge is?" he asked.

"It's right next to room 118. The door on the right as you face the classroom," the teacher replied.

Clay turned on his heel and raced for the stairs. She had to be there. She just had to be. He'd dropped her off at the front door. Where else could she be?

He nearly stumbled down the stairs in his haste and then raced along the hallway to room 118. He opened the door next to the classroom and was immediately assaulted by the smell of old coffee and tuna fish.

Two women sat at one of the three circular tables and there was no sign of Miranda. "Have either of you seen Miranda Silver this morning?" he asked.

They both shook their heads negatively. The alarm that Clay had tried to contain exploded in his chest. There was only one more place left to look. He headed for the gymnasium that doubled as a lunchroom.

He'd been in the gym once, when he and a couple of other cowboys had come to watch a basketball game. It was approaching noon and the smell of tacos filled the air.

He whirled into the room where tables and benches were filled with students enjoying their meals. The noise level was near deafening as several teachers and lunch monitors walked among the tables and tried to shush the students.

His eyes desperately scanned the crowd, but Miranda wasn't there. She wasn't anywhere. He left the lunchroom and leaned weakly against the hall wall.

All evidence pointed to the fact that she'd never made it into the school. And that meant she'd been gone for almost an hour and a half.

He took his phone out and, with shaking fingers, dialed Dillon's number. The lawman answered on the second ring. "She's gone, Dillon." His voice cracked with emotion. "She's gone and we need to find her."

Terror ripped through his body as he hung up and went to the school's front door to await Dillon. The only reasonable answer was that Miranda had been waylaid by somebody before she reached the front door of the school.

They must have somehow forced her into a vehicle and driven away before anyone had even seen her. A wave of helplessness swept over Clay. He didn't even know where to begin to search for her. And most terrifying of all, he didn't know if they were already too late.

* * *

Her head hurt.

Her mouth was dry.

Her eyelids were so heavy.

But an internal voice was screaming in the back of her brain. *Miranda, wake up. Danger! Danger! You have to wake up now.*

Was she back in the hospital? Or had she never left? Was her time with Clay, her love for Clay only some sort of a hallucination due to whatever drugs the doctors might have given her? What was happening? What was going on?

Miranda, you have to wake up. Open your eyes. The internal voice grew more insistent. *You are in trouble. You have to wake up.*

She managed to crack open an eyelid. She quickly closed it and frowned. Nothing made sense and her head hurt so badly. She cracked open an eyelid once again. She certainly wasn't in a hospital.

Wh… Where was she? The layer of cotton that had wrapped around her brain slowly began to unfurl. She'd been at the school…but she hadn't gone inside… Henry! Henry had been hurt! No…no, that wasn't true. That had been a lie, a horrible lie.

Lori.

The name thundered in her head and she gasped. Her eyes snapped open as the rest of the cotton fell away. Sunshine attempted to flow through a nearby dirty window, the end result a gloomy twilight in the unfamiliar room.

She was seated in a chair in a kitchen she'd never seen before. Wooden cabinets were half-painted while the refrigerator and stove looked like they belonged in another century.

The room smelled musty and in one corner a large web hung from the ceiling with a large spider awaiting its next prey. It wasn't until she tried to reach a hand up to rub her forehead that she realized she was tied to the chair.

Oh, God. Her arms were tied tightly to the armrests on either side of her. Her legs were bound to the front chair legs and a thick rope also wrapped around her waist, assuring that she wasn't going to stand up or get away no matter how hard she tried.

Panic leaped into her throat, momentarily making it almost impossible for her to breathe. Despite the tightness of the ropes around her wrists, she jerked on them and gasped when there was no give.

The top of the table where she sat was bare, as were the countertops. There was nothing to use to even attempt to cut the ropes and nothing to use as a weapon even if she could get her hands free.

Once again a terrific panic shot through her. Where was this place and how could she escape it? Was anyone else in the house? Was Lori here? Was Hank? Oh, God, was her ex-husband really behind the attacks on her? How could he do something like this? Why would he do this to her?

She drew in her breath and listened. She didn't hear anything. She expelled her breath. Wherever she was, she was apparently alone right now.

Once again she yanked up on her arms, hoping to feel a bit of give in the ropes, but to no avail. She pulled on her legs, but the bindings were simply too tight for her to escape.

She was stuck in this chair, in a small kitchen in a place she didn't recognize. How much time had passed since Clay had dropped her off at the school?

What had been in that syringe Lori had stuck in her? Had she been unconscious for minutes...for hours...for an entire day? Was the twilight semi-darkness of the room not because of a dirty window, but because it really was twilight?

Did Clay even know she was in trouble? Oh, God, how was he ever going to find her? Lori hadn't even been on their long list of suspects and Miranda had insisted to everyone that Hank would never do anything to harm her.

Hank. Was this his final betrayal of her? To kill her and take her away from their children forever? Why would he do such a thing? Had Lori talked him into being a part of this? Did Lori want her children?

Her chest clenched tight with pure terror. What

was going to happen to her when somebody returned to this place? Whatever it was, it wouldn't be good.

She finally did the only thing she knew she could do. She threw back her head and screamed.

Chapter 12

Clay was beside himself with fear. It hadn't taken Dillon long to arrive at the school, begin questioning people there and confirm that nobody had seen Miranda inside the building. He also checked on Robby, who was where he belonged in class and had been there since school started.

"We need to get the word out that she's missing," Clay told Dillon with panic eating his insides. "The more people looking for her, the better." He grabbed Dillon's arm. "We've got to find her, Dillon. We both know she's in deep trouble."

Dillon covered Clay's hand on his arm. "We're going to find her, Clay." Clay released his grip on

Dillon. "Why don't we head to the café? That's the best place to get the word out and start a search fast."

Clay followed Dillon there, his heart thundering so loudly he couldn't hear the roar of his truck's engine. What could have happened to her? Where could she be?

Dammit, who wanted to harm Miranda and now had the chance to do so? Acid rose to the back of his throat. He felt like throwing up, he wanted to fall to his knees and weep, but he knew he had to remain strong. He had to be strong for Miranda. He felt like tearing apart the entire town until they found her.

A killing anger rose inside him. If this person laid a finger on her, Clay would kill him. He clenched his hands tight around his steering wheel and imagined he was squeezing the neck of whoever had Miranda.

Clay had never been a violent kind of guy, but when it came to what was his and what he loved, all bets were off. Who in the hell was behind this?

It was imperative that they figure out who it was so they'd have an idea of where to look for her. Tears momentarily blurred his vision. They had to find her, and she *had* to be okay!

They reached the café. Thank God Mondays were always busy as people came out to eat and talk about the weekend past. The more people he and Dillon managed to contact quickly, the more people who would go out searching for her.

Clay walked in before Dillon. It was noisy with

the clatter of silverware and plenty of conversations filling the air. "Hey everybody," Clay yelled loudly to be heard above the din. "Hey," he yelled even louder to get everyone's attention.

People stopped talking. Forks remained poised between plate and mouth as everyone turned to look at him. "Miranda Silver has gone missing. I think she's in trouble." To his horror his voice cracked and his knees buckled.

Dillon grabbed him by the upper arm. "Go sit down. I'll take over."

Clay saw Mac and Flint in a booth. Mac stood and motioned for him to join them. Clay made his way there as Dillon began to explain about Miranda going to the school but never making it inside.

"I need anyone with information to come forward. If you saw anything at the school or anywhere else that involved Miranda this morning, come talk to me privately. I'll be just outside."

As Dillon left the café, a dark-haired woman Clay didn't recognize followed him. He started to get up, but Mac stopped him.

"What can we do to help?" Mac asked. "I can summon all the men at the ranch. What do you want them to do?"

"I'm not even sure what to tell you," Clay said with a sense of helplessness. Oh, God, he was in a nightmare and he couldn't wake up.

He'd vowed to keep her safe and somehow he'd

failed. Dammit, he should have waited and watched a little longer when he'd dropped her off at the school. He should have walked her inside and to the office.

"Clay?" Flint's voice pulled him from his thoughts.

"Why don't you all start searching the abandoned barns and sheds in the area," Clay said. Now wasn't the time to dwell on self-recrimination. He needed action.

Miranda had obviously been kidnapped by somebody and that somebody would need a place to hold her. At least within the next couple of hours they would be able to rule out all the abandoned buildings in the area.

He couldn't think about the very real possibility that she was already dead and it would be her lifeless body that might be found in one of those empty barns.

He got up from the table at the same time Dillon stepped inside and motioned for him. Clay hurried to the lawman. "I've got a lead. A woman was at the school at the same time you were and saw Miranda get into a dark-blue sedan with a rusty back bumper. She didn't get the license plate, but she said a dark-haired woman was driving."

Clay looked around. "Where's the witness? Who is she?"

"She wants to stay anonymous for now," Dillon replied. "At least if what she said was true then we know what kind of car we're looking for and that a woman was driving it."

Clay's mind whirled. A dark-haired woman? "It has to be somebody Miranda trusted. Otherwise she wouldn't have gotten into the car." He thought of all the dark-haired women he knew and the few that he had dated, but none of them made sense for what had happened.

Lori.

The name screamed inside Clay's head.

"It sounds like Lori's old Ford," Dillon said, obviously on the same wave length. "She doesn't drive it often, but I've occasionally seen her in it around town."

"It's Lori, Dillon. I don't know why she hates Miranda so much, but we both know it's her."

"I'm heading over to Lori and Hank's place now."

"You want me to ride with you or follow you?" Clay asked urgently. They couldn't be wrong about this. It had to be Lori. It just had to be, and if that was correct then they needed to get to Hank and Lori's place as soon as possible.

"I'd prefer you wait for me here," Dillon said as he headed in the direction of his patrol car.

"Well, you know damn well that's not happening." Clay quickly followed him and slid into Dillon's passenger seat.

As Dillon took off, doubts began to creep into Clay's mind. What if they were wrong? What if it wasn't Lori and they were wasting time on a wild goose chase?

What kind of a witness in this small town wanted to stay anonymous? Had it been the dark-haired woman who had followed Dillon out of the café? Who was she? Why had she been at the school? What if she was working with the real kidnapper and had intentionally thrown them off track?

He released a deep, pent-up sigh of anxiety. He didn't even want to voice any of his doubts out loud. He didn't want to give them substance by speaking them. It had to be Lori. It just had to be.

He leaned forward against his seat belt, as if by doing so he could make Dillon drive faster. The quicker they got to Hank and Lori's place, the faster they'd hopefully have some answers.

Was Hank involved in whatever was going on? Clay touched the butt of his gun as he thought of the man Miranda had once been married to.

"You realize that if Hank's involved with this then you're going to have to stop me from putting a bullet into his cold, black heart," Clay said tightly.

Dillon shot him a dark glance. "You'd better control yourself. I've got enough going on and I shouldn't have to worry about you committing murder. I swear Clay, if you give me any trouble then I won't hesitate to handcuff you to the back bumper of this car."

Clay knew Dillon would follow through on his

threat. He leaned back in the seat and drew several deep, long breaths in an effort to tamp down the rage that had been building inside of him.

Rationally he knew he wasn't going to shoot Hank, only because he didn't want to spend the rest of his life in jail. Dammit, he wanted to spend the rest of his life with Miranda. He could only hope that she was in Lori and Hank's house and she hadn't been harmed. Yet.

The house was located at a dead end. As they approached it, a burst of adrenaline seared through Clay. "No macho crap," Dillon said. "I'm going to knock on the front door. I don't want to do anything that might screw up a criminal case against them."

By that time they had pulled into the driveway of the small rental home. Clay flew out of the car and nearly ran to the front door, then he turned and waited for Dillon.

An urgency filled Clay's veins, a sick urgency. He needed to see Miranda right now. He needed to see her safe and sound. He waited impatiently as Dillon knocked on the wooden door.

"Lori? Hank? Is anyone home?" Dillon knocked again, harder this time and the door creaked open a couple of inches. They waited a moment. "They don't seem to be home," Dillon said.

Clay moved closer, hoping to get a peek inside. His heart beat loudly in his ears, but not so loudly that he didn't hear a deep moan from inside the house.

"Did you hear that?" he asked Dillon. "Somebody is in there and it sounds like they're in pain."

Clay wanted to burst through the door. It was only the fact that Dillon was in front of him that held him in place. Another faint moan came from inside.

"Do something, man," Clay cried frantically.

"I'm going inside to do a wellness check," Dillon said. He pulled his gun and opened the door to allow both men to enter into a small living room. There was a blanket and a bed pillow on the beige sofa, but nobody was sleeping there at the moment.

"The bedrooms," Clay whispered, as if Dillon was a novice and needed instructions. Clay pulled his gun as he followed Dillon down the hallway. His heart beat so fast he thought he might suffer a heart attack before they got through the house.

Dillon whirled into the first bedroom, his gun leading the way. Clay could tell by the fall of his shoulders that nobody was in the room.

He motioned Clay to follow him into the next small bedroom. It was also devoid of human presence. There was only one bedroom left, and Clay gripped his gun firmly as the two men approached the doorway.

Dillon stepped in first and muttered a curse beneath his breath. As Clay entered the room behind him, Dillon holstered his gun.

The room smelled of sour sweat and booze, and Hank was in the center of the double bed clad in a dirty white T-shirt and a pair of boxer shorts. He was obviously drunk as a skunk. Clay also holstered his gun.

"Hank, where's Lori?" Dillon asked.

Hank's bleary eyes opened to slits. "Go away," he slurred.

"Hank, we need your help. Where is Lori?" Clay stepped closer to the bed. He wanted to shake the man.

"Lori? She's…she's…" Hank frowned and closed his eyes.

"For God's sake, you stupid drunk. Lori has kidnapped Miranda. We need to know where she might have taken her," Clay exclaimed as he lost all of his patience.

Hank's red-rimmed eyes opened and he stared at them in bewilderment. "Lori kidnapped Miranda? Why would she do that? That's terrible." He began to weep, drunken tears that rolled down his cheeks. "Oh, God, why?"

"Hank, for God's sakes man, pull yourself together. We need your help," Dillon said. He looked at Clay. "See if you can find the stuff to make a pot of strong coffee."

Coffee? They didn't have time for coffee. Still, Clay left the room and headed for the kitchen. He'd make coffee and pour it down Hank's gullet in an effort to sober him up. He'd do it because right now the drunk in the bedroom was their only potential chance to find Miranda.

Miranda was exhausted. She had no idea how much time had passed, but she'd spent that time pulling and tugging on the bindings that tied her to the chair.

She'd cried and she'd screamed until she was breathless and hoarse, but it was obvious that, wherever she was, there was nobody nearby to hear her cries for help.

Now she sat quietly, trying to regain the strength she'd spent. She needed to remain strong. She needed to be ready in case a chance for escape came.

However, she couldn't stop the voice of doom that whispered in her ear. *It's too late. There is no rescue coming. You're never going to see your children again.*

She'd been so stupid in getting into Lori's car. She should have never trusted anyone, considering what had happened in her life. *And now you're not going to get to raise Henry and Jenny,* the voice continued to whisper.

She tried to silence the voice by telling herself that even if Clay wasn't in love with her, he'd be out looking for her. He'd be tearing down the town in an effort to find her. But would he find her before Lori and possibly Hank returned to this place… wherever it was?

Why, oh, why had this been done? What had she done to deserve this? A dog barked nearby. It sounded like a big dog. It barked for only a minute or so and then was silent. She suddenly tensed as she heard the click of a key in what she assumed was the front door, followed by a displacement of the air as the door whooshed open.

Oh, God. Her stomach muscles clenched tight as terror shook through her. Footsteps approached and Lori appeared carrying several bags.

"I had to drive into Clutter Creek to pick up a few things," she said and set the bags on the counter.

Clutter Creek? The small town was about an hour away from Bitterroot. So, where exactly was she? "Lori? Why are you doing this?"

Lori began to unpack food from one of the bags. Miranda watched her, her fear still huge inside her. "Lori…why?"

Lori whirled around and her pretty features contorted with anger. "Shut up. Shut the hell up. Can't you see I'm busy? I don't want to talk to you right now." She turned back and continued to put items away.

Miranda watched her with a renewed sense of helplessness. She'd hoped that maybe she could talk some sense to Lori before things went too far…

before anyone got hurt. "Is Hank in on this with you?" she couldn't help asking.

Once again Lori whirled around with a murderous expression on her face and a large knife in her hand. "I told you to shut up. If you don't keep quiet right now I'll take this knife and gut you like a fish."

Miranda sucked in a breath. The venom in Lori's voice and the malevolence on her face made her believe Lori might very well follow through on the threat.

She watched silently as Lori put a small container of milk and a package of cheese into the refrigerator. She then placed a couple of microwavable dinners in the freezer.

How long was she planning on staying in this place? How long did she intend to keep Miranda here? What exactly were her plans for Miranda?

When Lori began to unload the second bag of items, Miranda grew even more confused. New hardware for the cabinets, a hammer and nails and a couple of screwdrivers. After unpacking that bag, she reached beneath the sink and pulled out a can of paint.

A wild hysteria filled Miranda. What was Lori going to do? Force her to update the old wooden cabinets? Somehow she was pretty sure that wasn't why Lori had brought her here.

As the minutes ticked by and Lori refused to say a word, Miranda wanted to scream. The tension inside her built to the point that she felt as if she was about to explode.

Finally Lori pulled out one of the kitchen chairs. Miranda couldn't look at the woman's face. Her full attention was focused on the sharp, gleaming knife Lori held. "Now I'm ready to talk to you." Her tone was conversational, almost pleasant.

"D… Did you throw the acid at me at the carnival?" Miranda asked, even though she already knew the answer.

Lori shook her head ruefully. "Definitely a bad throw." She tossed the knife from one hand to the other. "I meant to throw it on your face and burn your features. I also cut your brakes and screwed with your air bag on your car."

"Why? What have I ever done to you?" Miranda tried to keep the fear out of her voice, but it was difficult with Lori passing the knife from hand to hand.

"You've never done anything to me personally. I'm doing this for me and Hank."

"I… I don't understand," Miranda replied.

"As long as you live, he'll never really be all mine."

Miranda stared at her. "But you already have Hank," she protested. "He lives with you. He loves you. There will never be anything between me and Hank again. I… I'm in love with somebody else. Just let me go now and I won't tell anyone what happened. No harm, no foul, Lori. Just let me go and take me back home."

"I can't do that. I need you gone." She stood and Miranda tensed. She began to pace in front of Miranda's chair. "I wanted to disfigure you with the acid, but that missed. Then I was hoping by cutting your brake line you'd hit something so hard it would kill you, but that didn't happen, either. You've been very difficult to kill, Miranda."

"Where is this place?" Miranda asked, hoping to tamp down the growing sick energy that had begun to waft from Lori. She needed time, and the only way she might survive this was to form some sort of a bond that would make her more difficult to kill.

Lori stopped pacing and a smile curved her lips. "This was my grandparents' house. When they died I took it over and have been renting it out. My last renters moved out a while ago and left a mess behind. You see, this is my alibi. I shopped in Clutter Creek and I have the timed receipt to prove it, then I spent the next two days working here to get the place ready to rent again." She smiled again. "I was here with my dog. Did you hear him bark? Hank hates old Duke, but Duke loves me. He'd kill for me. Anyway, so I've been here all day and knew nothing about your kidnapping."

"Where, exactly, is here?" Miranda asked. As long as they were talking, then nothing else was happening. If there was any chance that help might be coming, it was vital she keep Lori talking.

"Fifty miles away from Bitterroot and this cabin is nestled in a stand of trees that keeps it invisible from the road. I'm out of Bitterroot's county and the house is still registered in my grandparents' name. Nobody is going to find you here, Miranda."

A new wave of hopelessness swept through her. "Were you close to your grandparents?"

"Not really, but I was grateful that they left me this place. It's been paid off for years and so any rent I get is just pretty much spare money in my pocket. And it takes a lot of money to stay with Hank and keep him happy."

"What about him? Does he have anything to do with this? Does he know about this place and that you brought me here?"

"Hank has nothing to do with this, and he'll never know what happened to you. Nobody will know," Lori replied.

"Does he know about this place?" Miranda repeated.

"He's been here a couple of times, but if you think that gives you a chance of him rescuing you, think again. He was drunk both times he came out here with me. And when Hank is drunk he can't find his way out of a paper bag. He wouldn't be able to get here without me."

"Where was he when you left to kidnap me?"

"He was in bed and drunk. I made sure he was good and drunk before I left the house."

"Lori, you don't have to do this. For goodness' sakes, think about the children," Miranda said.

"I have thought about them. I know they are going to be heartbroken when you're gone, but with time and with my love, they'll eventually heal. I love them, Miranda, and I'll make sure they're okay."

Her words only further shattered Miranda's heart. Her children would be raised by a murderer. Eventually they would forget all about Miranda, but what happened if they angered Lori? Would she make them disappear, as well? Oh, God, she desperately needed rescue.

"You don't have to do this," Miranda repeated. "I'm telling you Hank loves you. He's with you," she said in a desperate effort to make the woman see the reality of the situation.

"Yes, he's with me." Her eyes narrowed ominously. "He sleeps with me, but he obsesses about you," she spat. "He talks about you all the time. He worries about you as if you two were still a couple. I've never hated a woman like I hate you."

"I'm sure his worry is because I'm the mother of his children," Miranda replied. "He just worries about the kids."

"No, no…it's you. And things won't be right until you're gone."

Miranda fought against the scream that rose in

the back of her throat as Lori moved closer to her. "And now I'm going to tell you how things are going to go," Lori said.

She tightened her grip on the knife, her hand shaking in obvious rage. She leaned close to Miranda, her face right in front of Miranda's.

"You'll be with me here the whole afternoon and then, when dusk falls, I'm going to kill you and bury your body in a hole I've already dug out in the pasture."

She raised the knife and placed the tip against Miranda's cheek. "And if you're wondering how we're going to spend our time together, then I'll tell you. I'm going to do a little painting on the cabinets, and I'm going to hurt you before I kill you."

To prove her point, she dragged the knife blade down the side of Miranda's face. Miranda screamed in pain as warm blood ran down her cheek.

Oh, God, she needed to be rescued. She begged for help to get there as soon as possible. She had no idea what time it was and how many hours she'd have to endure Lori's torture before dusk and death finally arrived.

Chapter 13

Precious minutes had ticked by...minutes that had turned into almost an hour. Hank now sat at his kitchen table, a cup of coffee before him and his head in his hands.

Clay and Dillon had dragged him out of bed and into a cold shower in an effort to get him more alert. Then they had begun to ply him with the coffee.

"I can't believe this. I just can't believe that Lori would do something like this," he finally said and raised his head. He lifted the coffee cup and took a drink.

When he lowered his cup, tears were in his eyes. "How long have you all been trying to sober me up?"

"Long enough," Clay replied tersely, impatiently.

"How do you know for sure it was Lori who took Miranda?" Hank asked.

"A witness saw Miranda get into Lori's car," Dillon replied. "Now, are you sober enough to tell us where Lori might possibly have taken Miranda?"

Clay moved closer to Hank. "Think, man. She already tried to throw acid on Miranda and jacked with her car in an effort to kill her. Miranda is in real trouble and you're our only chance to save her."

Clay had barely been able to contain himself over the last hour. He'd wanted to shake the drunk right out of Hank. During that time he'd received several phone calls from the Holiday Ranch cowboys telling him what barns and structures they had searched. But so far everyone was coming up empty-handed.

He had made a painful phone call to Katherine to see if she could meet the kids after school and take them to her house. Knowing how tight the two women were made it excruciating to tell her that her daughter was missing.

He couldn't even think about the kids and what might happen to them if they never found Miranda. Thoughts of Henry and Jenny threatened to break his heart thoroughly. They had to find Miranda and she just had to be okay. If nothing else, she needed to be okay for their sakes.

It was now all up to Hank. If he didn't have a lead for them, then they had just wasted an hour of search time. "Hank, you have to have something for us," he said desperately.

Hank frowned. "Maybe the rental place."

"What rental place?" Dillon asked. At the same time, a new burst of adrenaline filled Clay.

Hank's frown deepened. "It belonged to her grandparents and it's out in the country about fifty miles from here. Her last renters left it in a mess so she's been going out there to clean things up." He looked at Clay and then Dillon. "That's where she would go. That's where she would take Miranda."

"Do you know the address?" Dillon asked.

"I don't," Hank replied miserably. "And I think it's still in her grandparents' name and I don't know those names, either."

"Have you been there before? Could you take us there?" Clay asked.

Hank frowned again. "I've been there a couple of times, but I was fairly drunk when I went." The man had the grace to look ashamed. "Still, I think maybe I could get us there."

"Then let's go," Clay said.

He was the first one in Dillon's car. He sat in the back seat so Hank could ride up front and give directions. Hank had to get them there. He just had to. So much time had already passed. Too much time.

The other two men climbed into the car and Dillon headed for the highway that would take them out of town. Clay's heart beat painfully in his chest.

It seemed like it had been days since he walked into the high school in search of her. Were all their efforts too late? Would they get to Lori's place only to find Miranda dead?

He squeezed his eyes tightly closed. No. No, they couldn't be too late. Miranda couldn't be dead. She just couldn't be. If she was, Clay would forever be altered. He would never, ever love anyone like he loved Miranda. She just had to still be alive.

He opened his eyes and stared out at the passing scenery that went by in a blur of misty tears. Dillon's siren screamed, moving other drivers to the side of the road so they could speed ahead.

Clay only wished he knew what they were rushing to find. Would the woman he loved to distraction be dead or alive? Would they be in time to save her?

Nobody spoke as their car ate up the miles, and with each mile Clay's desperation grew bigger. Dillon drove fast, but it wasn't fast enough for Clay's comfort. Once again he found himself leaning forward against the seat belt, as if by doing so he could make the car go faster.

They had been driving for about thirty minutes when Hank told Dillon to slow down. "I know we make a right-hand turn on one of these country roads coming up ahead," he said.

Dillon slowed the car. "And once we make that right turn, how far is it to the cabin?"

"Maybe five miles or so. It's got a lot of tree cover."

Dillon silenced the siren. "There's no need to announce our arrival before we've assessed the situation," he said. "When you're sure we're close, Hank, we'll park and walk in quietly."

Clay was fine with that plan. Hopefully, with the element of surprise on their side, they could get in and rescue Miranda before Lori knew what was happening.

"Turn right," Hank said suddenly as they almost passed a dirt road.

Dillon made the turn and Clay's heartbeat accelerated. He didn't even want to think about the possibility that Lori hadn't brought her to the cabin, that they were on a wild goose chase that would end in nothing.

"Wait…wait," Hank said when they had only driven a short distance down the road. "This is wrong. This isn't the right turn. We need to go back."

"Jeez man." Clay punched the back of Hank's seat in frustration.

"Sorry, I'm doing the best I can here," Hank replied. Clay remained silent as Dillon turned the car around and got back on the highway.

They passed another turnoff to the right but Hank told Dillon to continue on. Did Hank really know where he was taking them? If he'd been drunk each time he'd been here then how accurate could his directions be?

As they approached another dirt road to the right, Hank told Dillon to turn off. "Go slow," he said. He leaned forward in his seat. "This looks right," he said. "I just know this is right." He sat up taller.

Clay prayed he was correct. If Clay didn't get to Miranda in the next ten minutes he thought he might die. Panic clawed up his throat. Sweat dotted his brow. His need for her was greater than anything he'd ever experienced before in his life.

"You might want to park now," Hank finally said. "The cabin is up ahead on the right."

"Are you sure?" Dillon asked.

"I'm pretty sure."

Clay was out of the back seat before Dillon came to a full stop at the side of the narrow, tree-lined dirt road. He and the other two men met in front of the car.

"We go in quiet and assess the situation. We don't want to do anything that might make the situation worse. I'll lead the way. Hopefully there are enough trees to provide us cover so we can get a look at the place and then figure out our best move," Dillon said.

Together the three walked up the road. Let this be it, Clay prayed. And let us be in time to find her alive. The words were a mantra as the three approached the overgrown driveway to the cabin.

Staying behind a stand of trees, they got their first look at the cabin. From the outside, the place looked completely abandoned. The paint was weathered to a dull gray and the wood siding sported more than its share of rot. Weeds and brush grew tall, as if trying to hide the eyesore of a cabin.

Still, his heart momentarily lifted from dark despair when he spied Lori's car parked at the side. She was the last person to be seen with Miranda and he hoped like hell Miranda was in that old cabin with her.

They got closer, and all of a sudden a big Rottweiler stood from where he had apparently been sleeping on the porch. A thick chain tethered him to a porch railing. He appeared on alert and then, to Clay's horror, he began to bark wildly.

A window at the front of the cabin flew open. "Whoever is out there, go away. There is no trespassing on this property so get the hell off it," Lori yelled out.

Dillon stepped from behind a tree. "Lori, I just want to talk to you," he called out.

A gun fired from the window. Clay gasped in surprise as Dillon dove for cover.

"I told you to go away. I'm busy working on this place and I don't have time for socializing," Lori said.

"I'll only take up a few minutes of your time," Dillon replied.

"I don't have a couple minutes to spare." She fired off another shot.

Oh, God, this was all going sideways. Clay really hadn't considered Lori would have a gun and wouldn't be afraid to use it.

"Is Miranda in there with you? We know she got into your car," Dillon shouted back.

"I don't know what you're talking about," Lori replied. "I've been here all morning working."

"A witness saw Miranda get into your car at the school this morning," Dillon said.

"Lori, honey, if you've got Miranda in there with you, then just let her go," Hank yelled.

"It's all about Miranda. It's always all about Miranda," Lori screamed in obvious rage. The gun exploded again. "Go away, and if anyone even thinks about entering this cabin, there will be hell to pay and you won't like what happens."

"Lori, don't you see that it's too late?" Dillon said. "If Miranda is still alive then let her go and you won't be facing murder charges."

"All I want is Hank's love. I love him more than anyone else will ever love him, but Miranda always came between us. He was either drunk or obsessing about her and there wasn't anything left over for me," Lori said.

"That's not true, honey," Hank replied. Dillon nodded, as if to keep Hank talking to her. Once again Clay felt that the fate of the woman he loved hung in the balance of a drunk and his dysfunctional relationship with the woman in his life.

"You know I love you, Lori. I never loved Miranda as much as I love you," Hank yelled. "All Miranda is to me is the mother of my children. Other than that she means nothing to me."

"Just tell us if Miranda is in there and if she's alive," Dillon said.

Once again, the gun fired. "I don't want to talk to you, Dillon Bowie. The bitch is alive, but she's not as pretty as she used to be."

Oh, God. Clay's stomach clenched tight. He didn't give a damn what Miranda looked like, but what had Lori done to her? How bad were her wounds?

"Let her go, Lori and we'll figure this all out," Dillon said.

"Come on, honey. Why don't you come out and let's get back to living our life together," Hank said. "If you kill Miranda, then you'll go to prison for life and we'll never be together again."

His words were followed by a long silence and the only sound in the air was the ominous growl of the dog, who bared his teeth as if ready to attack. Clay's nerves were strung so tight they actually hurt beneath his skin. This standoff with a crazy woman in control of Miranda's life was killing him.

"I just wanted it to be you and me, Hank," Lori finally shouted out the window. "I thought if she was gone then things would be better between us."

"If you just walk out here I promise things will be different…things will be so much better between us," Hank replied. "Honey, I didn't know you felt this way. Come on out and we'll fix things. Lori, you have to know in your heart that I love you to the moon and back."

"You mean it, Hank? Things will really be different between us? You'll stop talking about her? Stop even thinking about her?"

"I promise things will be different," Hank replied.

Nothing happened for several gut-wrenching moments. Clay held his breath as finally the door creaked open. Was Lori really going to just walk out? Was Miranda dead or alive? If she was alive, what had Lori done to her?

Lori appeared in the doorway with her hands held up and open. "Go to her," Dillon said to Hank. "Get her away from the cabin."

Hank stepped out from behind the stand of trees where the men had been standing. "Honey?" He took several steps forward and opened up his arms. "Come on, baby," he urged. "I really need to hug you right now."

She ran to him with a joyous expression on her face, but when Hank had her in his arms, he handed her right to Dillon, who handcuffed her, kicking and screaming at Hank for betraying her.

Not wanting to take a chance with the dog by

going in through the front door, Clay ran around to the side of the house to find another way in.

Terror nearly closed off the back of his throat. What was he going to find inside? Had Lori already killed Miranda so he would find her dead body on the floor? Or had she been tortured so badly he'd find her bloody and broken?

He picked up a rock near the foundation and smashed the first window he came to at the back of the house. "Miranda," he yelled as he climbed through the window. There was no answer.

He entered a small, empty bedroom. He raced into the hallway and paused, unsure which way to run. "Miranda!" Her name tore from the very depths of him. He paused and listened. He thought he heard a muffled cry coming from the kitchen area. He raced in that direction and when he reached the room he gasped in shock.

Miranda was tied to a kitchen chair, a dirty rag shoved into her mouth. It wasn't the sight of the thick ropes around her body or the gag that made him gasp. Rather, it was the blood that ran into her eyes, half-blinding her, and the blood that dripped down the side of her face and made a horrible splatter pattern on her white blouse.

He fell to his knees in front of her, crying as he pulled the gag out of her mouth. "Miranda…oh, God, are you all right? What in the hell did she do to you?"

"I'm okay...just...just untie me," she said between sobs. "Get me out of this place."

Clay was vaguely aware of Hank entering the room. "Oh, God, what did she do? What can I do to help?"

"Hand me that knife." Clay gestured to a knife on the counter. "And then call for an ambulance."

Hank handed him the knife and Clay grimaced as he saw the bloody edge. Lori must have used it to cut up Miranda's face. "Thank God you got here," Miranda said through her tears. "She was going to kill me, Clay. She...she was going to kill me at dusk and bury me in a hole in the pasture where I'd never be found again."

"That's not going to happen now or on any other day." He wanted to check what was beneath all the blood on her face, but he was afraid to do anything with that until a doctor took care of it.

"It's all going to be fine now, Miranda," he said as he sawed at the ropes that held one of her wrists to the chair. "Lori is going to prison for a very long time and that danger is gone forever." He managed to get one wrist free and started on the other one.

Her entire body trembled as she continued to cry weakly. "Sh...she did it all, Clay. She threw the acid and...and she cut my brake lines. She hated me. She wanted me dead."

"Shh, honey, I know." He got her second wrist

free and by that time Dillon had joined them. He gasped when he saw her bloody features.

"Where is she?" Miranda asked in alarm, her eyes wide with terror.

"Don't worry, Miranda. She's handcuffed and locked in the back of my patrol car," Dillon replied. "Believe me, she's not going to escape."

"Could you help me with the rest of these ropes?" Clay asked. "And she needs to see a doctor as soon as possible."

With both Hank and Dillon's help, Miranda was finally free of the bonds and she threw herself into Clay's arms and began to weep again. Clay did his best to soothe her and it wasn't long before an ambulance arrived.

She disappeared into the back of the vehicle to be treated and Clay waited outside for her. Several county patrol cars arrived and the officers got out of the car to speak to Dillon.

Clay was sick with worry over Miranda. The nasty cuts on her face were obvious, but had Lori hurt her someplace where it wasn't obvious? He didn't think she had any broken bones, but he couldn't be sure.

Dillon spoke to the ambulance driver and it was agreed that he would take her to the Bitterroot hospital for an additional checkup.

Clay started to climb into the back of the vehicle to ride with her, but she stopped him. "Ride back with Dillon and make sure Lori doesn't somehow get away. You can meet me at the hospital and then Dillon wants me at the station for more questioning." She released a deep sigh. "Right now I just want to rest." As if to prove her point, she closed her eyes.

Once again, she looked small and achingly vulnerable on the gurney. There was nothing he wanted to do more than crawl up next to her and listen to her heartbeat against his, an assurance that she was really and would be okay.

But he had to abide by her wishes. He left the ambulance more than a little bit disturbed that she hadn't wanted him with her for the ride.

Now that the danger was really over, was this the beginning of her distancing herself from him? Was it possible her love hadn't been real, that knowing she was safe, she didn't need him anymore?

Miranda sat on the end of an examining room table and tried not to cry out with pain as Dr. Johnson stitched up the knife cut on the side of her face. The forehead cut had required only butterfly bandages.

"Thank goodness it was a clean cut," Dr. Johnson said. "It was easy to close up and I don't think it will leave you with much of a scar. Facial wounds are always scary looking because they bleed so much."

He finished his work and then leaned back in his chair and stared at her intently. "And now, how are you doing emotionally? You know, if you need somebody to talk to, I can get you in to see Ellie."

Ellie Miller was an older woman who was a psychiatrist. Even though she told everyone she was retired, she occasionally saw patients from an office in her home.

"No, that's not necessary, at least, not right now. All I really need is to get back to my normal life." She drew in a deep breath. She wasn't even sure she knew what a normal life looked like anymore. All she knew was that she didn't have to live in fear anymore.

Remembering the look of horror on Clay's face when she'd confessed her love for him shot a new pain through her heart. She supposed he'd be eager to move out now and get back to his real life. She no longer had to be a burden to him.

"I'll need to see you again in my office in about ten days to remove those stitches," Dr. Johnson said as he helped her down from the examining table.

"I'll make an office appointment tomorrow morning," she replied.

What she'd really like to do right now was see Henry and Jenny. After believing she would never see them again, her heart ached with the need to hold them close and kiss their sweet faces. But first, she needed to see Dillon at the police station and get this whole ordeal behind her once and for all.

She walked out into the waiting room to find

Clay. He stood as she entered the room and smiled in obvious relief. "There's that beautiful face," he said.

She raised a hand to the gauze that covered her stitches. "Not so beautiful anymore," she said ruefully.

"As long as you can smile, you're beautiful," he replied.

She gave him a wan smile. "Let's get to the police station so I can be done with all this and get home to my kids."

"What time is it?" she asked once they were in his truck.

"Just after five," he replied.

"If felt like I was tied to that chair for days." She released a weary sigh. "And I've never been so terrified as I was with Lori. I now feel like I could sleep for days."

"Do you want to wait to meet with Dillon? If you're too tired you can always do it tomorrow. I'm sure he would understand, considering the trauma you've been through."

She shook her head. "No, I'd rather get it over with now."

"I've got to tell you, I've never been so afraid in my life. We would have gotten to that cabin a lot sooner if Hank hadn't been drunk." Clay explained to her about sobering up Hank enough that he'd finally been able to help them.

He glanced over at her. "Can we take a minute

and talk about us? I want you to know that I'm in love with you."

His words ripped through her, and at that moment she realized she was angry with him. Where had his love been when she bared her soul to him earlier in the day? The look of horror on his face when she'd professed her love for him was burned into her brain. "I really think what we need right now is a little distance from each other."

"A little distance?" He parked in front of the police station, shut off the truck engine and turned to look at her.

"I think it's best if, when we get home, you pack your bags and get back to your life at the ranch. I really want to get back to my own routine."

He stared at her and in the depths of his gaze she saw pain. "I don't understand. You told me you loved me this morning, and now I'm telling you I'm completely and totally in love with you."

"Clay, I really don't want to get into this now. I've had a really long, traumatic day. This is the last thing I need right now." She didn't wait for his answer but got out of the passenger door and headed for the police station.

She didn't believe in the love he had just declared to her. He hadn't shown or said anything about loving her that morning and the only thing that had changed since then was that she'd been kidnapped and cut up. She was sure what he felt about her now was pity and a relief that he'd helped save her life.

Dillon was waiting for them in his office and the two of them sat in the chairs facing his desk. "I need to know exactly what happened. Why did you get in the car with her?"

She explained about Lori using Henry getting hurt as a ruse. "If I'd really thought about it, I might not have gone with her. The school has always called me if one of the kids are sick or whatever. But Lori was so convincing, and I panicked, and all I could think about was getting to Henry as soon as possible."

Dillon took notes as he continued to question her. She told him about the syringe and how whatever had been in it had knocked her out cold. As she remembered waking up and knowing she was in trouble, she began to tremble.

Despite what she'd said to Clay in the truck, he reached out and took her cold, shaking hand in his big warm one. Her heart squeezed tight at his show of support.

She also told Dillon about Lori attempting to set up an alibi by shopping in Clutter Creek. "She was so cunning...and so crazy with hatred."

She reached up and touched her bandages. "She was very matter-of-fact when she told me she was going to work on the cabinets and torture me throughout the day and then she was going to kill me at dusk."

"You don't ever have to worry about her again, Miranda. She'll be charged with enough crimes that she will never see the light of day again," Dillon assured her.

"Are we about done here?" Clay asked. "I know Miranda is eager to get home and I've got some things to do there before I can call it a night."

There was such sadness in his voice and Miranda knew she'd put the sadness inside him. But she was so scared that his love for her wasn't real. She'd rather they parted ways now than continue on to the point that he would eventually realize it wasn't really love he felt for her, and then he would leave her and it would only rip her apart even more.

His confession of love had come too late for the party and now she had to stay strong, do the right thing and let him go.

"Before you two leave, the witness who saw Miranda get into Lori's car wants to talk to you. She's waiting in the conference room," Dillon said.

Clay exchanged a curious look with her. Why did she want to speak to them now? Clay had told her the witness wanted to remain anonymous.

Certainly Miranda wanted to thank her for coming forward. Without her, the odds were good Miranda would be dead right now. "I'd love to get the chance to thank her," she said.

"Me, too," Clay agreed. "She saved the woman I'm in love with." He looked longingly at Miranda.

She looked away. "Let's go see who this woman is." She stood, as did Clay, and together they followed Dillon down the hallway. He gestured for them to enter the conference room where a dark-haired stranger sat at the table.

She rose as they entered and a tentative smile curved her lips. She was beautiful, with a heart-shaped face and piercing blue eyes.

"Hi, I'm Rachel Jones." She held out her hand to Clay. He shook it, but she didn't release her hold on him. "I used to be Violet Madison."

Clay yanked his hand away from her as if he'd been electrified and Miranda drew in a deep breath of stunned surprise as she realized she was looking at Clay's mother.

Clay stared at the woman who had walked out of his life when he had been eight years old. Myriad emotions battled inside his head, inside his heart. Part of him wanted to storm out and not give her the time of day, but another part of him desperately needed some answers from her.

He jammed his hands into his pockets and stared at her. Despite the passing of time and the fact that her hair was dark instead of blond, his heart remembered her features, her beautiful blue eyes and the loving curve of her lips. He could smell the familiar scent of violets that wafted from her, a scent that pulled forth happy memories of when she'd been in his life.

"What are you doing here?" he finally asked.

"Can we all sit down and talk?" she asked.

"Maybe I should just wait outside," Miranda said.

"No," he protested. "Please…" He pleaded with his eyes. "Please stay." He didn't think he could get through the emotional scene ahead without her. Surely she could give him that much.

She nodded and sat at one of the chairs at the table. He sat next to her and his mother sat across from them. He was angry enough at her that he didn't even want to look at her, and yet some part of him hungered to stare at her familiar features and remember how she'd once made him feel so loved.

"I've been in town several weeks now," she began. "I… I've been following you. I followed you this morning when you took Miranda to the school and that's how I saw her get into Lori's car."

"Why have you been following me?" he asked.

"I had been trying to get up the nerve to talk to you. Clay, I understand if you don't want to hear anything I have to say, but there are some things I'd like you to know."

He crossed his arms over his chest. "And what if I don't want to hear them?"

"Then I'll go away and never bother you again." Her eyes dimmed a bit with her words.

"I'm here and I'm listening," he said grudgingly.

"I… I don't even know where to begin," she said.

"How about you begin when you just disappeared from my life?" His heart squeezed tight and pain soared through him. He unfolded his arms and placed them on the armrests. He was surprised and comforted when Miranda grabbed his hand and held on tight.

"That night I tucked you into bed as usual and then your father nearly beat the life out of me. He told me if I tried to leave him he would kill me…and I believed him. I also believed that if I stayed with him, he'd end up killing me anyway. That night I told him I had to get some clothes from the line, and when I stepped outside, I just kept walking. Without thinking, without any plan, I left." The words were spoken quickly, as if she'd been thinking of this moment for a very long time.

"And so you just decided to leave me with that abusive man," Clay accused.

Violet's cheeks flushed with color. "In all the time I was with your father I never saw him lay a finger on you. It never entered my mind that he would ever be abusive to you."

"Yeah, well, when you left things changed."

Tears appeared in her eyes. "When I left that night my plan was to come back for you."

"So, what happened?" he asked, and Miranda leaned closer to him. "Please… I need to know why you left me there." Tears were thick in his throat and he swallowed hard against them.

She told him about hitching a ride to Oklahoma City where she found a shelter to stay in at night. During the day she lived on the streets. She had been there only a few days when she developed pneumonia and wound up in the hospital for two weeks. During that stay she was also diagnosed with PTSD and anxiety disorders.

"I was in no shape to come and get you, either physically, mentally or materially. I had no place to live and wouldn't have even been able to provide you a meal. And I was absolutely terrified that your father would find me and carry out all this threats." For just a moment she looked haunted.

Clay wanted to hate her. He wanted to resent her. He told himself to get up and walk out of the room, but instead he remained seated and felt her pain and grief wafting through him.

"I wound up at a battered women's shelter where I finally started to rebuild my life," she continued. She reached a hand up and touched her head. "I dyed my hair in an effort to stay hidden from your father and I worked at a hamburger joint. Once I'd earned enough money, I bought a car and got a tiny, crappy apartment on the wrong side of town."

She gazed at him with such love it half-stole his breath and stroked the wounds that lay deep in his heart, deep in his very soul.

"I was slowly rebuilding my life, but I missed you so badly. I finally got up the nerve to go see you. I showed up at one of your baseball games. I cheered every time you hit a ball or made a catch."

"Why didn't you let me know you were there?" he asked. Once again Miranda squeezed his hand tightly, silently giving him support.

"I couldn't, not with your father right there. Besides, you looked so happy when I watched you. What right did I have to walk back into your life? I had nothing to offer you. There were days the only meal I ate was the free one I got at the burger place where I worked. You looked happy and well-adjusted, and so I decided to leave you be. But the hardest thing I've ever done in my life was drive away from your ballgames and know it would be another week before I dared see you again."

"The ball field was the only place I was happy because it was the only way I got to escape for a little while from the abuse I suffered."

She began to weep, and a touch of forgiveness edged into his heart. They had both been victims of a brutal man.

"When you ran away, I… I didn't know how to f…find you," she said through her tears. "Y…you were just gone."

"How did you find me here?" he asked.

She swiped at her cheeks and straightened in her chair. "Social media. Several weeks ago you and your friends made a large contribution to help horses and it came up in my feed. There was a picture of all of you with your names. But I didn't need your name. The minute I looked at your photo I knew you were my beautiful baby boy and so I came here."

"And now that you're here, what do you want?"

She searched his features, as he did hers. "I'd like a place in your life. That's why I wanted Miranda here for all this…because it's obvious the two of you love each other, and if you allow me into your life then I'll also be entering Miranda's."

A new pain ripped through him. He knew how he felt about Miranda, but he wasn't so sure how she felt about him now. The short conversation they'd shared before coming in here had taken him completely by surprise.

"I know it will take time," his mother said. "I'm willing to take whatever you're willing to give me. I want to be in your life. I need my little lightning bug back in my life and I hope that some healing will begin."

Once again Clay searched her features. She still had the beautiful blue eyes he remembered although they now held a wealth of pain. Hadn't they both already hurt enough?

"The healing has already begun," he finally said. It was true. Forgiveness felt so much better than bitter anger. There was still a hurt little boy inside him, but time would hopefully help heal him.

"I want you in my life," he said and joy leaped into her features. "Right now as we sit here, I'm not sure what that will look like, but we'll figure it out. But, right now I need to get Miranda home. She's been through a traumatic day and I know she wants to get home to her children."

"Of course." Violet got up from the table. "Can I call you tomorrow?"

She and Clay exchanged phone numbers and then she was gone. He stood and pulled Miranda to her feet. "Sorry about all this," he said.

"Don't be sorry. It was a wonderful thing," she replied. "I don't know about you, but I believed every word she said. She always loved you, Clay, and it's obvious she still does."

"I believe that, too," he replied. He had lost so many years with her, but hoped they could build a new relationship as adults.

Although he still found it hard to believe that the reunion had happened. How lucky were they that his mother had reentered his life in time to be part of saving Miranda's life? Fate, or whatever, had been on their sides.

They walked out of the police station and got into his truck, and his thoughts turned to the woman next to him. There was no way he was going to let her out of his life without a fight. He wasn't about to lose the one woman who had captured his heart completely.

The ride back to her house was a silent one. He

knew she was exhausted, but there was one last thing that needed to be addressed before she got the children home and she went to bed.

He waited until they walked into her house and then he placed his hands on her shoulders. "If you think I'm going to just pack my bags and leave, then you're sadly mistaken. I love you, Miranda, and I want to spend the rest of my life loving you."

"I have never loved you more than when I saw you find forgiveness in your heart for your mother," she replied, her eyes simmering with emotion. "But Clay, are you sure you're not just saying you love me because you pity me?"

He looked at her in shocked surprise. "Why would I pity you?"

Her gaze was troubled as she raised a hand to the bandage on her cheek. "I might be left with a scar."

"I don't give a damn about a scar," he scoffed. He ran his thumb down the side of her face that wasn't bandaged. "If Lori would have poked out your eyes, then I would have been your sight. If she cut off your ears, then I would have been your hearing. I fell in love with you, Miranda, not your face. Although I still find looking at your face more than a little bit pleasant."

"But when I told you I was in love with you this morning, you looked horrified by the very idea. Then after you rescued me this afternoon, you professed to love me."

"I don't profess anything. You shocked me this morning and it took me several minutes to process that you were on the same page I was. I went back to the school to tell you I loved you, but you weren't there."

He pulled her close against him and wrapped his arms around her, tears burning his eyes as he thought of the moment he'd realized she was gone. "I've never been so scared. I was crazed with fear until I walked into that kitchen and saw that you were alive. We belong together, Miranda. Don't you feel that in your heart? In your soul?"

She stepped back from his embrace and his heart crashed to the ground. Was she still going to send him away?

"Does this mean I get to be the boss all the time?" she asked with an impish smile.

"Oh, no," he laughed as his heart soared. "It's fifty-fifty all the way now." He drew her back into his arms. "Do you remember once I told you I always keep my promises?" She nodded and he continued, "I promise right now to love and honor you for the rest of my life."

"And I promise to do the same," she replied.

"Then I think this moment calls for a kiss." He lowered his lips to hers in a kiss that silently confirmed his promise and she kissed him back with a passion that stole his breath away.

Epilogue

It had been two weeks since Miranda had been tied up and tortured by Lori. The stitches had been removed from Miranda's face and the wounds were healing nicely.

She now stood at her living room window and watched Clay playing catch with Henry and Jenny. Her heart swelled with happiness…a happiness that greeted her each morning when she awakened in Clay's arms.

He'd gone back to work at the ranch during the days but returned to the house after his work there was done. The kids were delirious with Clay's presence in the home. He filled it with his deep, infectious laughter, and at night he thrilled her with his kisses and lovemaking and plans for their future together.

She straightened as she saw Hank's familiar pickup. He parked at the curb and got out of the truck. They had seen very little of him in the last two weeks. He hadn't even taken the children for his weekends with them.

He greeted Clay and the two men shook hands, then Clay gestured toward the house and Hank walked up to the door.

She opened the front door and ushered him inside. "You're looking a lot better than the last time I saw you," he said.

On the other hand, Hank looked like hell. His eyes were swollen and red-rimmed, and his features had grown gaunt since the last time she'd seen him.

"Do you mind if I sit and talk to you for a few minutes?" he asked.

"Of course I don't mind." She led him into the living room where he sat on the edge of a chair and she sank down onto the sofa.

"I swear I didn't know," he began. "Miranda, you have to believe me, I had no idea what Lori was up to." Tears began to ooze from his eyes. "I would have stopped her. If I'd only known about her plans, I would have tied her to a kitchen chair and turned her in to Dillon."

"Hank, I believe you," she replied softly. "Is that

why you haven't come around lately? Why you haven't taken the kids on the weekends? Because you were afraid I'd think you guilty of something?"

He nodded as huge gulping sobs overtook him. "If I hadn't been drunk so much of the time I might have known what she was up to. Someplace in the back of your mind you have to be blaming me, too."

"Hank, please pull yourself together," she replied. "I don't blame you for anything that woman did. She was sneaky and none of us thought it could be her behind the attacks. Even if you'd been stone sober, I don't think you would have known anything."

He swiped at his wet cheeks and drew in several deep, steadying breaths. He stared at her for a long moment and then sighed. "I'm glad about you and Clay. I'm glad that you found a man worthy of your love. I want you to be happy always, Miranda."

"I know that, Hank. And I wish you'd find some happiness for yourself."

He stared at her once again with his tortured eyes. "I'm not just a drunk. I'm an alcoholic and I came to tell you and the kids goodbye."

"Goodbye?" She looked at him in alarm.

"I'm driving down to Texas. There's a place there that has agreed to take me into their ninety-day program. I need to do this for the kids."

She smiled at him. "You need to do it for yourself. I'm so proud of you for doing this."

"Yeah, I feel pretty good about it." He stood. "I'm

all packed up and ready to hit the road. I just needed to stop by here and let you know what I was doing."

She walked him to the door. "Good luck on this new venture and you know we'll all support you here." He looked so vulnerable. She drew him into a hug. "Be well, Hank."

She released him and he smiled, the first real smile she'd seen from him in a very long time. "I'm going to be well."

Together they walked out the front door where Hank hugged the kids and told them how much he loved them but that he needed to go away for a little while.

He shook Clay's hand once again and then got into his truck and pulled away from the curb. When he was gone, Clay walked over to her and threw his arm around her shoulders. "Everything okay?" he asked.

"He's going to a rehab in Texas."

"That's good. You know I love your children, but they need their father involved in their lives," he said.

"Speaking of...aren't you supposed to meet your mother for lunch?"

He looked at his watch and gasped. "The morning got away from me."

"Go get cleaned up and get out of here," she said.

"Are you sure you don't want to come with me?"

She shook her head. "There will be time for me

and the kids to enjoy your mother's company eventually. But for right now, I think it's important you have more quality alone time with her."

In the last two weeks he'd met with Violet twice, once sharing breakfast at the café and the second time eating lunch together.

He now pulled Miranda into his arms. "Have I told you today that I love you?" He smiled down at her.

"You might have mentioned it, but it never hurts to say it again," she replied.

He reached up and framed her face with the palms of his hands. "I love you, Miranda Silver, and I can't wait to change your name to Miranda Madison. Tell me you're going to marry me and make an honest man out of me."

"I'm going to marry you and make an honest man out of you," she said with a laugh.

"Are you guys going to get married?" Jenny's voice turned them around.

"Are you?" Henry asked with excitement lighting his eyes.

"Yes, we are," Clay said. "And after we get married we're going to talk to your mom about getting you a baby brother or a baby sister."

As the kids cheered and danced around them, Miranda knew her heart couldn't get any fuller. Her children's excited laughter, coupled with the intense love shining from Clay's eyes, made her feel as if she were the luckiest woman in the entire world.

If Clay Madison was Romeo, then she was just glad that out of all the women in Bitterroot, she was his Juliet. When she looked into his beautiful blue eyes, she saw her future of love and laughter. She saw her future with him filled with tenderness and passion. Finally she saw her dreams of the kind of family she'd always wanted coming true.

When he leaned down and took her mouth with his in a sweet, tender kiss she knew she was going to love this cowboy for the rest of her life.

* * * * *

Don't forget previous titles in the
Cowboys of Holiday Ranch series:

Guardian Cowboy
Sheltered by the Cowboy
Killer Cowboy
Operation Cowboy Daddy
Cowboy at Arms

Available now from
Harlequin Romantic Suspense!

Scarlett's voice broke and she looked down, valiantly
struggling to regain emotional control.

Travis could no more have remained in his chair than he
could have stopped breathing. He took a few steps and dropped
down beside her, then gathered her in his arms and held her.

Like before, his body instantly responded to her softness.
And like before, he kept his desire under control. "I'm sorry,"
he murmured, allowing himself the pleasure of caressing her
back and shoulders. "I can only imagine how much that hurts."

"And now I'm facing losing Hal before I even get to know
him," she continued. "Worse, we have no idea what we're
battling, so it's difficult to get together a cohesive defense."

He managed something that he hoped sounded like assent.
She wiggled slightly, nestling closer to him. Desire zinged
through his veins, and he had to shift his body so she wouldn't
recognize his growing arousal.

How could this tiny woman make him desire her without
even trying?

HRSEXP0319

"Travis?" She tilted her face to look up at him, her lips parted. "Would you do me a favor?"

At that moment, he would have promised her the moon. "I'll try," he answered. "What is it?"

"Would you kiss me again?" she breathed.

Just like that, she managed to rip away every shred of the armor he'd attempted to build around him. With a groan, he lowered his mouth to her, claiming her lips with a hunger that tore through and gutted him.

Rock hard, he could barely move, never mind think. While he wasn't entirely sure she knew what she was doing to him, he knew if she kept it up, he'd lose the last shred of what little self-control he'd managed to hang on to.

"Scarlett," he growled.

She must have heard the warning in his voice, because her hands stilled. Though she didn't move away from him, not yet. And she had to, because right now the only movement he felt capable of making would be ripping off their clothes and pushing himself up inside of her.

"We need to stop," he made himself say.

"Do we?" Pushing slightly back, she gazed up at him, her lips swollen from his kisses and her eyes dark with desire.

Don't miss
Texas Ranch Justice *by Karen Whiddon,*
available April 2019 wherever
Harlequin® Romantic Suspense books
and ebooks are sold.

www.Harlequin.com

HRSEXP0319